His Healing

His Guardians
Book 1

by

Ronna Bacon

Ps 30:2
LORD my God, I called to you for help
and you healed me.

Ps 147:3
He heals the brokenhearted and binds up their wounds

Table of Contents

His Healing

Prologue

He watched from the hillside as she struggled to rise from the ditch. His diabolic chuckle echoed through the stillness of the dusk. She was down and no one was around to help her. He looked at the sky. The rain clouds were moving in and soon the cold night would be shrouded in fog and rain. He had no pity for her. She deserved everything that came to her. He glanced her way once more. She was laying still, unable to rise. Her bicycle lay in a crumpled and twisted heap near her. She was on her own.

He turned and walked away. Justice, as far as he was concerned, had been done. It is said the sins of the father are visited on their children. Nor in his family, but in hers. Her father had taken away something very precious to him. He would seek until he found it once more. Now that she was out of the way, he would be able to search her home for what he needed that he was sure she had.

Looking back, the darkness had dropped, covering the site of his deed. He laughed once again as he strode heavily away, overcoat flapping in the wind that was arising, driving the chilly rain into pellets of ice. By morning, she would be dead, and he would   be   able   to   take   over.

Chapter 1

Lieutenant Doug Foster, commander of the Riverville Emergency Task Force, dropped onto the booth seat at the back of his Uncle Mac's cafe. It was early Saturday morning, and he couldn't figure out why he was up and out so early. Saturdays were usually days he could sleep in a bit and then spend the day puttering around his yard and house. But here he sat, two of his buddies with him. Dave Callahan, a paramedic and friend since childhood, sat across from him, engrossed in reading the menu that he knew by heart, fingers tapping absently on the plastic-covered paper. Doug took a look at the third member of their group. Matt Cahill he was just beginning to get to know. Matt worked on his cousin's Abe security team and for once was home on a Saturday. The three had agreed to meet that Saturday morning to go rock climbing.

Matt looked around the cafe, taking in what was happening around him and noting the few customers seated around the building. His glance slid to the outdoors and he watched as a younger woman stepped down from a service van and walked towards the door. He could tell she was tired just by the way she moved. Her jeans and denim shirt looked dusty and stained and he wondered how that could be so early in the morning.

Doug looked up as the door opened and lifted his hand to the woman as she entered. She detoured towards the counter and then headed their way. Doug slid out off the bench seat so she could slide in beside him. Matt wondered at that, but then he mentally shrugged. Maybe this was God telling him to lighten up a bit, that things didn't have to be so rigid.

Dave slid the menu back behind the napkin holder as Mac began placing their orders in front of them. Matt noticed that the woman, he still had to learn her name, only had toast and juice.

Doug looked over at him. "You've never met Sarah yet, have you?" At the negative shake of his head, Doug made the introductions. "She's also my next door neighbour."

Sarah Devlin. Now that was a name that belonged over the seas on the Emerald Island, he thought. Curly below the shoulder dark brown hair that she had back in a ponytail and hazel eyes complimented the faint sprinkling of freckles over her nose. Closer up, he could see the exhaustion in her face, as well as something else he couldn't put his finger on.

Sarah's phone rang but she ignored it. As it continued to ring, Doug reached over and tugged it out of her back pocket with an ease that said they were old friends.

"It's John," he stated.

"I know. That's his ringtone."

"Aren't you going to answer it?"

She shook her head. "I've already send him a text message. I'll catch up with him later."

Her phone rang again.

"He's not going to give up, you know?" Doug was baiting her.

She shrugged. "It's not that important."

Doug shook his head and then answered her phone. "Sarah's phone. She's here, John, but she said she doesn't want to talk with you." A sparkle of mischief peeked out of Doug's eyes. "John wants to know if you're okay and if the inspection is still on schedule for this morning."

She took her time chewing her mouthful of toast, took a swallow of juice, and then looked at Doug. "Tell him it's inspected, signed off, and the old geezer has his keys."

Matt choked on his coffee at her words. Looking at her, he would never have expected that to come out of her mouth. Dave started to laugh as Doug repeated her words, then looked at her, eyes round.

"John wants to know how you managed that?"

She shrugged. "I had some very nice policemen company in the form of the chief and his deputy, as well as a few others. The inspector was there since 4 o'clock yesterday afternoon, working right behind us as we finished at 5 o'clock this morning."

Doug listened to John again and then asked, "John wants to know how you got Mr. Benson out there at that time of the morning."

She stared at Doug. "Easy. I told him if he didn't, then the nice men of the Emergency Task Force would show up at his door at 5:01 a.m. and that

I would also buy a billboard to air his dirty laundry.”

By this time, Dave had his head on his crossed arms on the table, shoulders shaking with mirth. Matt stared at her, not quite sure if she was serious or not.

Doug finally convinced John that the work was done, what work Matt was still trying to sort out, and handed her back her phone. “You’ve made an enemy there, Sarah.”

“He already knows I can’t stand the sight of him and would love to see him taken down.” She looked at the three men staring at her. “You know the history, Doug, and why I can’t stand him. Now, if you will excuse me, I’m heading home.”

Before he stood to let her out, Doug laid his hand on her arm. “How many hours have you worked this week?”

“Not going there, Doug. You’re not my boss. I wanted that job done and so did John. It’s done, inspected, and he can’t stop it now if he tried.”

Doug refused to move, and it turned into a staring contest between the two. Dave watched, eyes alight with laughter, wondering who would win this time. Matt’s brown eyes flicked between the two, not quite sure what was happening.

Sarah finally sighed, knowing Doug wasn’t going to budge this time. Every once in a while, she had to let him win their contests.

“Too many, Doug, way too many. Clark and I pulled 60 hours straight, Andy and Pete came and worked the overnight hours as well.”

“Sarah.”

"Don't start. John finally had to hire security for the site, and one of us had to be on site all the time. We had sabotage going on. I finally pulled the schematics, the signed and witnessed agreements, and our lawyer and I paid his lawyer a call. He backed off then." She gave Doug a shove and he stood. She walked away without a backward glance, fatigue showing in the very way she moved.

Matt watched as she walked across the parking lot, a limp evident by now. His brows creased in thought, he didn't see Doug and Dave study him and then follow his line of sight to Sarah. They shared a glance and then looked down at their plates.

"She's been up and down too many ladders in the last few days," Dave commented.

"She has at that." Doug pushed his half-eaten plate of food to one side, unable to continue eating. "She won't take it easy, no matter what's she told."

Dave agreed. "No, she won't. With John and Meg away because of Meg's grandmother being so sick, she's picked up her pace. John won't be pleased." Dave stared at Doug. "Maybe you should call and talk to him."

Doug looked over at Matt, who was studying his plate as if to decide whether he had had enough. "Sarah was in a really bad accident a couple of years ago, Matt. A hit and run." Matt looked up, having a good idea of what was coming. He was the paramedic on their security team. "She lay for hours in the cold rain and bitter wind before someone found her. She had been biking and someone ran her down and left her there. She ended up with a broken hip and to this day has problems if she's over tired or has over exerted herself."

Matt flinched. "She was just left there?" At their nods, he fought to compose himself. "They have no idea who?"

"Not really. Sarah doesn't make enemies. She collects people, is what my Mom used to say, she has so many friends. But she is really picky as to close friends, and if you get to be a close friend, then you know you are that important to her." Doug hesitated, not sure how to frame his next words. "I think Sarah has a good idea who it was but she has never said anything. The investigation is still open."

Dave stared through the window. "I still don't understand, though, why she chose her line of work. There are easier ways for a woman to make a living."

"Sarah has never been known to back away from a challenge. When John told her she couldn't be an electrician because she's female, she set out to prove him wrong."

"An electrician?" Matt wasn't sure if he had heard them right.

Doug nodded. "She works with her cousin. They took over her Dad's company when he retired and moved from here."

Matt stared out the window to where her van had been parked. He just didn't understand women going into trades. His gaze shifted, and then his eyes narrowed. He watched as a man walked away from the spot where Sarah's van had sat, looking down at something in his hand. Suspicions high, he memorized as much as he could about him. He shuddered, suddenly feeling evil in the area.

Later that afternoon, Peg Brown handed Doug a plate of brownies as she stepped into his kitchen. Eddie, Peg, and Doug quite often got together on a weekend to share a meal, and today Dave and Matt had joined them. Eddie had stopped to check the grill before going over to talk with Matt and Dave.

Peg looked around. "Sarah's not here?"

Doug shook his head. "I'm not sure she will be. We saw her this morning, and she was exhausted. She said she had put in a lot of hours on Benson's building."

Peg nodded as she stared across the yard at Sarah's home. "That's what Eddie has said, He's been around there at times, making sure she was okay. I'm glad they're finished with it. I know Sarah never wanted to take it on."

"What's the history there, Peg?" Doug leaned back against the counter, crossing his arms, and searching his aunt's face. "There's something there, and Sarah has never said what."

Peg looked at him, then looked away. "It's not mine for the telling, Doug. If and when Sarah wants you to know what happened in the past, she will tell you. It involves her father, that's all I will say." Peg moved towards the door. "If she was that exhausted this morning, then she has to have been hurting too. I'm heading over to see how she is."

Doug stared at the door after she closed it, then turned to stare at his friend's home, trying to figure out what the story was. He saw that Peg had Matt with her. Good, he thought, she won't argue as much with him as she would with Dave, if she needs some help.

Chapter 2

Peg tapped at the door and then keyed in an access code. Matt stepped in behind her. He liked the comfort of Sarah's kitchen, uncluttered countertops, and warm autumn tones. He reached for the work boots she had dropped in the middle of the floor, and looking around, set them tidily on the boot tray near the door. He could hear Peg moving through the nice-sized bungalow, looking for Sarah.

"Sarah, dear, it's Peg." Peg didn't see Sarah in her bedroom and turned back to the living room. She could see where Sarah had been sitting, an open bottle of now-flat ginger ale sitting on the table beside a large easy chair and her medication bottle beside it, a soft cream blanket thrown back from where she had wrapped it around herself. A now-warm ice pack sat on the chair arm. Peg moved on towards the office, then stopped. She dropped to her knees beside Sarah.

"Sarah, dear, you really shouldn't be sleeping on the floor."

At those words, Matt followed Peg's voice and stood just out of Sarah's sight. He watched as Peg touched Sarah's shoulder.

Sarah moved slightly, grimacing in pain. "Peg. What are you doing here? What time is it?"

"It's suppertime, Sarah." Peg searched Sarah's face, then quickly glanced at her body. She seemed to be okay other than groggy. "What are you doing on the floor, my dear?"

"I figured it would be easier if I was already on the floor if I fainted." Sarah laid her head back down on her arm and closed her eyes, exhaustion still evident.

"You fainted?" Peg looked up as Matt moved closer and then squatted at Sarah's back. At Sarah's brief nod, Peg's face crumpled for a minute, then she composed herself. "Did you hurt anything?"

Sarah shook her head. "I don't think so. The pain was just that bad. I should have known better, shouldn't I? I just couldn't let him win."

Peg looked up to see Matt staring down at Sarah, eyes questioning what she had said. She reached over and touched his arm, shaking her head when he looked at her.

"I have Matt with me, dear. Why don't we get you up and see how you are once you're upright again?"

Sarah sighed. "I would rather just stay here. It's so much easier not to move."

Matt grinned as he listened to her. Feisty is the word he would choose to describe her. Peg caught his attention again and motioned for his help.

"Sarah, Matt's going to help you up. Do you want to be on your feet or back in your chair?"

"Do I have a choice? My choice would be to stay here."

Peg shook her head. "I gave you the two choices I'm allowing you. On your feet or in your chair. You pick. Though I must say, you could really use a shower. You and your clothes are filthy."

"Thanks so much, Peg. You make a girl feel pretty." She gritted her teeth and tried to push herself up but was lying on the wrong side to do so.

Matt spoke for the first time. "Sarah, I'm going to lift you. Don't try to help. Okay?" He waited but she didn't respond. He leaned over her so he could see her face. "Sarah, did you hear me?"

"You're just as bossy as Doug. I heard you."

Matt grinned again, then reached and carefully lifted Sarah to her feet. She flinched with pain as her right foot rested on the floor.

"Peg, I just don't think I can do supper tonight." Sarah was almost in tears from the pain.

Matt studied her face, then looked down at her foot. "You're hurting more than just from the hip. What did you hurt today?"

She shook her head and refused to look at him.

"Sarah, I'm a paramedic. I know you are hurting far worse than you should. What did you hurt?"

She refused to look at him, instead staring past him with a stubborn look on her face.

Matt sighed, then said, "Sarah, sometimes we have to accept help. God puts people in our lives to do just that. It's okay to want to hide and keep the pain away so it doesn't become a stumbling block to your friendships. But sometimes, God wants us to step down off the high horse we've put ourselves on and accept the help He has sent. He sent me to help you. Let me do that."

Peg drew in a sharp breath, knowing that those words would not sit well with Sarah and would have the opposite effect to what Matt wanted. He didn't know her well enough to know that. Then, amazed, Peg watched as Sarah's face softened, and then she gave a small nod.

"I'm sorry, Matt, you're right. I'm just too stubborn. I've always had to do things myself, at least for the last few years, and I hate being a burden on anyone."

"Sarah, I don't think any of your friends would consider you a burden. Just remember, we're here to help you. God wants us to serve one another, and part of the way I do that is to help, to use the skills He's given me." He stopped speaking, his hands lightly holding her upper arms to keep her upright, her hands on his arms, fingers tightened until they were white. "So, to go back to my question, what did you hurt and how?"

Peg watched in astonishment as Matt was able to break through and chop down barriers none of them had ever been able to do and that with just a few well chosen words. Her eyes narrowing, she glanced from Matt to Sarah and back again and then nodded. God was at work. He had to be for Sarah to give in so easily.

Sarah turned her head to look at Matt. "My muscles cramped in the hip. I thought I was okay, but when I went to go back to my chair, I fainted. I don't faint." A scowl crossed her face. "It must have been about 1 or so it happened."

"So you've been lying on the floor, watching the dust bunnies play for about four hours or so?"

She glared at him. "I don't have dust bunnies, buster."

He laughed, then said, "Okay, so where does it hurt?"

"I went down on the knee and then the hip."

Matt looked at Peg with a question on his face, and she nodded. "I'm going to help you to your bedroom, and then Peg will help you into something other than your jeans. If you won't go and have it looked at, then please, may I take a look at your knee?"

She shook her head. "No, I've been through this before. I just need to elevate it and ice it. Just go back to your supper and tell Doug not to come over." Holding onto the wall, she limped away from him as fast as she was able to.

Matt stood and watched, running his hand through his almost mahogany hair. Peg touched his arm and then moved past him to follow Sarah. He could hear quiet voices and turned back to the kitchen. After a while, Peg came out and drawing him with her, closed the door and reset the lock. Linking her arm with his, she led him across the lawn to Doug's.

"Will she be okay on her own?"

Peg hesitated, then spoke, "She refuses help, Matt, and we can't force her. For years, she has held people away from her. Ever since her accident, she has done that even more. It's like she's afraid someone will get hurt because of her. We have prayed for her so much about this, talked to her, but now all we can do is leave it with God. She working through issues surrounding that and some other things she has never spoken about."

"If I can help in any way, please let me know."

Peg patted his hand that was lying on hers. "You have, Matt. None of the rest of us would have reached her tonight. She would not have responded to us, just walked away from us. Somehow, what you said made a difference. Keep trying with her. I think you're the one God has brought into her life to help her get through the new few weeks."

Doug looked up as they climbed the steps to his back deck, then glanced over at Sarah's. "Sarah's not coming?"

Peg shook her head. "No, she says she needs to sleep more than she needs to eat. I'll check on her again before we leave to see if there's anything she wants."

Eddie pulled Matt aside as they were leaving. "Peg got a chance to mention that you reached through to Sarah where the rest of us haven't been able to."

Matt looked embarrassed. "I don't know how I did that, except it was God. He gave the words to me. There're not what I would have said myself."

Eddie nodded. "He does that. Peg and I, we think the world of Sarah even though she's not blood to us. Matt, don't take this wrong, but I think God has brought you here to reach her." Eddie stopped and studied Matt. "You have something going on in your own life, too, that you need to resolve. Let us help you.”

Matt studied the ground, then nodded. “I’ll think about it, Eddie.”

****

He stood on the neighbour’s front steps, as if he was waiting for them to answer the door, even though the house was dark. He watched as the vehicles left Doug’s, then his eyes turned to her house. There was faint light coming around the closed drapes. He would watch and wait. One day and one day soon, he would have what he wanted. She would not win.

Chapter 3

be Finlay studied the seven men seated around the conference table. Each man had their own skills, but together they made a strong team. He knew the upcoming security assignment would be a tough one and take them overseas to a war-torn country. He hated those assignments. There was always that chance that something terrible would happen. He would need to sit down with Murphy, he thought, his second-in-command, when they returned and evaluate where they wanted the team to go. He was getting tired of jetting off all over the world, and he suspected the team was as well. He had heard the rumblings that they would like to settle down somewhere and start family lives. This was now the time, he thought, to re-evaluate where they were needed.

Going over the new assignment took time. He could tell there were many questions and hesitations about it, ones he shared. He sent them off with the warning to make sure all the gear was ready, even though he knew it would be.

"Matt, got a minute?"

Matt stopped, then came back and perched on the table. "What's up, Abe?"

Abe studied Matt, taking in the calm exterior he presented to the world. Abe knew there was much that went on behind the serene face and that he was fighting battles he let no one know about.

"Eddie mentioned that you were able to get through to Sarah."

Matt shrugged. "Don't ask me how. I really don't know her, I had just met her that morning at breakfast."

Abe looked down at the floor as he thought about that. "God sometimes moves quickly when He sees the person He wants to use in the right place at the right time. I know that was how it was with you and Sarah." He looked up. "I know Eddie asked you to stay in her life and help her. I am too. Doug's my cousin and he and Sarah had been best friends for years. They're like brother and sister to one another. If I can help ease his burden of worry for Sarah, I would like to. I think you're the one we've needed for years to reach her."

Matt looked out the window and then said, "What happened with her accident? Doug mentioned a hit and run."

Abe nodded. "She had been out biking. She loved to be able to get out at the end of a day and just ride. Weekends would find her riding 20 or 30 miles and thinking nothing of it. That night, she was run off the road. The police found some evidence but they haven't said what it is, hoping to be able to apprehend someone for it. She lay there in the ditch, in cold, muddy water with a bitter wind blowing. It is a miracle she even survived that. Her right hip was fractured and they had to put in a plate and screws to repair it. That was the worst of her injuries." Abe stopped, trying to compose himself. "That night changed her life totally. She lost the freedom she treasured, the ability to do what she wanted. She became dependent on people for help and she is too independent a person to want that for long. She did have bitterness but worked through it. She hasn't said much as to how, but she has a peace about that night. Yes, she would like to face the person responsible and ask them why, but if it never happens, she's okay with that."

Matt shook his head. "Sometimes I just don't understand human nature." He stood to leave, then turned. "You're thinking about not taking any more overseas assignments, aren't you?"

Abe stared at him. "How did you know?"

Matt shrugged. "You're getting tired of all the traveling and everything that goes with the security details over there. If you decide just to do them in this country or area, I'm fine with that." He turned and walked away, leaving Abe staring thoughtfully after him.

How does he do that, Abe pondered. He seems to know what you're thinking before you even do. But he's so right. I need to sit down and work through what we do.

Sarah stood, leaning against Doug's kitchen counter as she watched him finishing off some paperwork. She was getting restless. She moved away from the counter and out onto his back deck.

Doug tapped the papers together into a neat pile and then locked them in his briefcase. His eyes went to where Sarah had been standing and then to the window across from him. Something was going on but he just couldn't put his finger to it. He stood and then stopped at the back door. Sarah was moving away from the house, towards her own. He had never seen the dejection before that he could see today in her posture, not even after the surgery. So what was going on?

Then, he remembered the date. It was two years ago today that her then boyfriend had walked away from her and out of her life, just a few short days after her accident. Doug remembered him standing in the hospital parking lot, telling Doug that she was damaged, that he didn't want her in his life. He studied his right hand. He could still feel the pain from his fist hitting that chin and sending the man to his back on the pavement. Despite the threats of being sued for police brutality, Doug stood over him, plainly telling him that he had just insulted his best friend, and if he really wanted to make something of himself, he should probably move to another town. Within two days, the man had packed up and left. Sarah had never spoken about that time in her life. Doug had no idea if she was still grieving or not.

Gideon Andrews, Abe's brother in law, met him just as he was leaving the conference room. He waved a sheaf of papers at him.

"Got a minute?"

"Sure." Abe turned and walked back inside, taking a seat at the table once again.

Gideon sat down beside him. "You know how you mentioned you were really uncomfortable with this assignment?" At Abe's nod, Gideon handed him the papers. "I think you should call it off. It's a set up."

Abe's eyes shot to Gideon, then back to the papers he held. He read through them quickly, then went back over Gideon's research. "No such person. No such group. We researched it. How did we not find this out?"

"It was hidden so well I almost didn't find it either. Sidney said something when we were talking about it, and that triggered a thought. It must have been God, Abe. If you go, you won't be coming back, nor will your team."

Abe sat back, his hand going to his chin. "You're right. None of us have felt good about this assignment. But who?"

"I'm still working on that angle. So is Sidney." At Abe's look, he held up a hand. "Don't worry. He's working on it himself and in his home office. We're not taking any chances there's another leak, not after what happened with the leak and Rebecca."

Abe stood and paced. "For a while now, I have considered giving up all overseas assignments. The guys are getting tired of travelling and I can't say I blame them. They're burning out that way. We can pick up enough around this country and this area alone to keep busy. I've been turning down requests." He turned, his eyes searching Gideon's. "And I know Rebecca worries when we're away."

Gideon nodded. "She does. And it's time to change the way your company is going. It was okay for your Dad and Uncle. They were two of them and they could divide it between them. There's just you and you need to step back and consider that one day you may be married and have a family. Do you want to put that aside just to make money or do you want to do what you would really love to do?”

“How do you do that, Gideon, reach right in and pull out thoughts I haven’t even firmed up in my mind?” Gideon laughed as Abe shook his head. Abe reached to shake Gideon’s hand. “Tell your wife we’re staying home and she owes us a big dinner.”

Gideon slapped Abe on the shoulder as he walked by him. “I will. She was already planning what she would cook.”

Abe stood in thought for a moment, then went to find the other seven members of his team. A sense of relief coursed through him. Yes, God had led Gideon to the knowledge they needed. But who was setting him up that way?

Matt knocked at Sarah’s front door later that afternoon. He liked the white wicker furniture she had on it with the flowered cushions, the rug on the floor, the planters of colourful flowers sitting around. He turned as the door opened and she stood framed in the screen door.

“What are you doing here? I thought you were flying out tonight.”

He shook his head. “Abe called off the assignment. There was a problem with it.” All of Abe’s team were very careful in how they talked about their work, giving few details. “I was wondering, seeing as I have the evening free, if you would like to have dinner with me.”

She stared at him. “Dinner? Really? I don’t know. Can I let you know tomorrow?” Her eyes began to sparkle with mischief.

“Sure, you can, as long as we have already had

dinner tonight."

She nodded, then opened the door. "Come in. I won't be long." She turned as he stepped through the door. "Oh, just be careful the cats don't get out."

"Cats?"

She nodded. "They're around here somewhere."

Matt watched as she walked away, then turned to look around. His eyes stopped as he noticed a beautiful black cat sitting on the back of the couch watching him, green eyes brilliant against the black. Then he felt something around his ankles and jumped. Looking down he saw a white cat with a marking on its back, soft blue eyes look at him. He looked harder at it.

"Sarah, your cat has a spider on its back."

"She does. It's quite the unique black marking, isn't it?" She appeared in the hallway, pulling on a sweater as she came towards him. "That's Spider. And over on the couch is Miss Muffet."

Spider? Miss Muffet? Okay, he thought, I can see Spider but Miss Muffet?

Sarah snickered as he stared at Miss Muffet, trying to figure out how she got her name. "I'll let you think about that one for a while."

****

He stood and watched as Matt closed the car door after Sarah was seated and then moved around to slide behind the wheel. He watched as they drove off, then turned to study her house. Somehow, he needed to get in there but she had too good an alarm system.

He had already tried that. She couldn't even have normal locks, having to have a keypad instead. He glared the way they had driven off and then moved to his own vehicle sitting in a neighbour's driveway. He would follow them. At some point, he would need to approach her and he knew that would be very difficult to do.

Chapter 4

Matt studied the menu in front of him, feeling unsure of himself, not a normal feeling for him. He had acted on impulse in going to ask Sarah out. That she had agreed so quickly surprised him. He raised his eyes to watch her. She was looking at him, an inscrutable look on her face.

"Okay," she stated, "which one?"

Matt's puzzled gaze met her. "What do you mean, which one?"

"Just what I said. Which one phoned you and told you to take me out to dinner?"

Matt smiled as he shook his head. "No one did. I came up with this on my own. Really, I did." His smile disappeared. "Did you think I would only ask you out to dinner if someone put me up to it? No, Sarah, I wanted to spend some time with you and dinner seemed a good idea."

She looked distressed. "I'm sorry, Matt. I'm just so used to people meddling in my life, thinking I need to be out and about, and that I need an escort." She sighed. "This was so Doug, that I figured he had called you."

"No, he didn't. Even if he had, I would still have come."

Mac set their orders in front of them, and with a

word of prayer for the food, they dug in.

"I don't know how Mac does it, but he knows what we want before we do."

Sarah laughed. "He's always been like that. He can't explain it either."

Matt watched as she suddenly stiffened. "Talk to me, Sarah. Who just came in?"

She shook her head. "No, it's really nothing. Just someone I don't like."

Matt watched her closer as she bent her head over her dinner. "I'll let it go this time, but never again. You need to trust me, Sarah. I'm not walking away from you. Ever."

She looked up at him then, searching his face and eyes, seeing the strength and security and courage that he radiated. She nodded. "At some point, Matt, I may tell you a story that not many people know. But it involves others besides me and I can't tell it without talking to them first."

"I can live with that, but if it comes down to your life being threatened or endangered, then this guarantee is off the table, and you will talk to me.

She sat back, startled at the tone of his voice and words. "We'll see, Matt."

He stared at her until she looked down, then said, "I don't want to force it, Sarah, but if it comes to it I will."

Abe sat at an adjacent booth with Gideon and Rebecca. It was nice, he thought, not to be overseas. It had been the right decision but something still niggled at him about it. Who had set him and his team up? He looked up as Rebecca touched his arm, and followed her eyes to where she was nodding. Matt and Sarah. Now that was an interesting couple. He knew Matt didn't date, wouldn't even ask a lady out for a causal meal with a group of friends, and here he sat, in the middle of town in a well-known cafe, with a beautiful lady. Rebecca smiled at him as he looked back at her and he just shook her head.

Matt walked Sarah towards his car, hand on her back. The parking lot had been full when they arrived and he had had to park near the back. As they neared his car, a dark form rose and came towards them. Matt shoved Sarah behind him and backed away from the man. As he backed away, he heard squealing of tires and spun to see a white car headed right for him. He wrapped Sarah in his arms and threw himself sideways, taking the brunt of the fall. His shoulder hit the pavement, then his head. Darkness swirled around him, as he faintly heard voices shouting, then nothing.

Abe heard the squealing tires and hit the cafe door on the run, heading for the scene of the accident. The car was long gone as was the man Matt had seen. His eyes searching the area, he dropped to his knees besides the forms. His heart dropped when he realized it was Matt and Sarah.

"I've called for an ambulance and the police." Gideon spoke over his shoulder. Then, moving around to the other side, he stopped. "No, it's not!"

Abe nodded. "Matt and Sarah. Sarah, just lie still. I don't want you to move until we have help."

Sarah had stirred and was trying to sit up. "What happened, Abe? Matt! Is he okay?" She pushed at Matt's arms trying to get free.

Gideon laid his hand on her. "Stay put, Sarah. We don't either one of you to move until we have help."

Gideon and Abe stood back as the paramedics worked on Matt and Sarah and then loaded their stretchers into the ambulances. Eddie approached.

"Someone said it was Matt and Sarah?"

Abe nodded. "They had been here for dinner and were headed back to his car by the looks of it. Witnesses say someone had come towards them, Matt moved back a few steps and then the car came at them. We're not sure if he was clipped or just went down."

Eddie studied the area of the accident and then swept a glance around the onlookers. "I'll have the patrol officers canvas and see if anyone saw much. But it's not likely."

Abe nodded, then turned to Gideon. "It's too coincidental, Gideon, to me giving up that assignment. Which one were they after? Matt? Sarah?"

"What do mean, Sarah?"

Abe turned to him with a questioning look. "You've heard about her accident? It's felt widely that it was not a regular hit and run but that she was targeted by someone. That someone Caleb says they have never been able to find or even figure out who it would be."

"I'll see what I can find out."

Sarah stirred, hurting all over. She turned her

head. Doug was sitting by her bedside, head back, looking as if he was asleep. She studied the man who had been her best friend since they were toddlers. She wondered that he had never found the special lady to share his life. She prayed for him, that he would. She turned her head and stared at the windows near her bed. The sun was coming up, sending beautiful pink rays into the lightening sky. Thank you, Father, that I am alive to see this day. She prayed for healing for Matt. He had taken the fall for her last night, wrapping her in his arms and keeping her safe. She needed to find out how he was. She wasn't told last night.

Her door opened and Caleb Logan, Riverville Police Chief and a good friend, stepped in. He slanted a look at Doug, then stopped by her bedside.

"How are you feeling?" He kept his voice low.

"Sore and ready to leave. How's Matt?" Her eyes pleaded with him to tell her.

"He's sore, like you, bruised, and has a whopper of a headache. He's not able to tell us much. Did you see anything?"

Sarah shook her head. "No. Matt all of sudden shoved me behind him and then we were stepping backwards. Next thing, he's taking me down and I can hear a motor roaring past us." She looked at Caleb. "Did the car hit him?"

Caleb shook his head. "No, he was able to avoid that, but he did knock himself out when he hit the ground." He watched her as he talked. He always felt there was more to what she had said about her accident two years ago but had never pushed her.

Now, he felt it was time to do so, but he would wait until she was home. "You'll both be going home today. Peg's waiting to take you home with her and Eddie."

Sarah shook her head. "No, I'm not going there. I'm going home."

"Sarah, that's not a good idea. We don't know if it was just a simple accident last night or if either Matt or you were the target. We need someone with you."

"No, Caleb. I'm not going anywhere but to my home. Now, get Doug out of here so I can get up and dressed."

Caleb hesitated, knowing she was going to run and that there wasn't a lot he could do about it. He roused Doug and taking him with him, left the room.

Sarah pushed the covers back, swung her legs off the bed and then hesitated. She really wasn't as brave as she let on. She let her feet touch the floor and grimaced with pain. She was moving slowly this morning but she wanted to be gone before someone came back for her. She dressed, then cracked the door open and peeked out. No one seemed around her door in the early morning activity. She blended in with the nursing staff and cleaning people and was gone by the time Peg reached her room. Peg stood, shaking her head. Yes, Sarah had run. She turned and headed for the elevator, then hesitated. She just couldn't barge into Sarah's home. She would have to wait, as much as it would hurt to do so.

Caleb looked up as Eddie tapped at his door and then entered. "She ran, did she?"

Eddie nodded. "She was gone before Peg got there. She must have slipped out just after you left. Something's going on with her and has been for years."

Caleb thoughtfully stared at Eddie. "There has been, and she won't talk about it. Now, we have Matt. Which one was targeted? Abe seems to feel that it may have been to do with the assignment he backed out of."

"What did Matt say when you talked with him?"

"Not a lot more than what we were told last night. He does remember a form walking towards them last night and stepping back. Not too much after that. We don't have anyone other than Matt and Sarah and whoever it was he saw." Caleb ran his hand through his hair. "I hope we don't have another one, Eddie. We've had so many already."

Eddie nodded. "Me, too, Caleb. Now that Ben's retired, that will make it more difficult to investigate. Other than Frankie, we don't have the trained officers that we need yet. They're good but they're young."

"If we have Frankie talk to Sarah, it might work. We just need to keep Doug away. He's pretty hot under the collar about them being run down."

Eddie stared at his hands, then looked up at Caleb. "Doug has always had a soft spot for her, going back to when they were little. He never let anyone pick on her. He sees himself as her older brother, and this time, that's not going to work. Matt is stepping in, whether he realizes that what he's doing or not, and Sarah is letting him do it, where she won't with any of the rest of us."

"That's an interesting statement, Eddie. I never thought I would see Sarah let a man step in like she has Matt."

"She doesn't. I don't think she knows Doug helped drive Tom away after her accident."

"What do you mean?" Caleb looked puzzled.

"You never knew?" Caleb shook his head, and Eddie continued, "We never knew until just recently. Tom confronted Doug in the parking lot of the hospital just a few days her accident. He told Doug she was damaged goods and he didn't want her any more. He ended up on the pavement, Doug ended up with a sore hand, and Tom left town a couple of days later and has never come back."

Caleb sat back. "I had never heard that. I wondered why he left town so quick."

"I let Doug know that it wasn't a good idea, but he just shrugged it off."

Caleb nodded. "I'll have a talk with him. If Sarah is a target, we'll need him to be very careful. I don't want to suspend him."

****

He stood under the trees in Doug's backyard, watching her house. He knew Doug was not home or he would not have been there. He had followed her as she came home in the taxi and then went into her house. He had not seen her since. One day he would confront her. Her high and mighty attitude would disappear quickly.

Chapter 5

Matt was restless. Abe wouldn't let him work until the doctor cleared him, and he wasn't used to sitting around. He looked up as Joseph neared him.

"You're going to wear a hole in the ground, you know," Joseph commented.

"Shut up, Joseph. I'm not used to this enforced quiet."

Joseph slanted a look at him. "I know. So how about we go see your girl?"

Matt spun around and stared at him. "I don't have a girl."

"Sure, you do. Let's go see Sarah."

Despite his protests to the contrary, Matt was glad Joseph had suggested the trip to town. His eyes constantly moving, he scanned the area around the compound and then on the road to town.

Joseph spoke. "We have a tail, you know."

Matt turned to look out the back window. "The white car?"

Joseph nodded. "The witness said it was a white car the other night. You game to stop and find out?"

Matt shook his head. "He'd be gone before we

even stopped. I'm just trying to figure out what's going on."

"What's going on is that either you or Sarah or both of you are targets." Joseph looked over at Matt. "You never say a lot about your early years, other than your Mom raised you after your Dad and brother and sister were killed."

Matt sat staring out the window and Joseph wondered if he had even heard him. Finally, he spoke. "No, I don't. I was young, 11, when my Dad was killed. A drunk driver who walked away with a few scratches. Our insurance company sued him and he lost big time. He also ended up in jail for a couple of years, lost his license for life. His family was very bitter towards ours. I've often wondered if they would ever track me down to retaliate."

"And you're just telling me now?"

Matt nodded. "Abe knows some of it but not the whole story. No one does. It just hurt too much to talk about, even now. Mom and I ended up having to live with her parents, and that was no piece of cake."

Joseph looked in the mirror once again. "Hold on, Matt. He's coming at a pretty good rate of speed."

Matt turned to watch. "He is." His eyes narrowed as he tried to make out details of the car. "Ready for some fun?"

"If you're up to it!" Joseph grinned. "I am."

Joseph watched as the car closed the distance, judging the speed of the other driver. As the car approached, he slowed and then spun the wheel, heading back in the opposite direction as the white car flew by. He once again spun the wheel, tires squealing in protest, and took off after the car. By the time he had turned, the car was gone. He pulled to the side of the road and stopped.

"He certainly didn't want to get caught, did he?" Matt commented mildly. "Think the cameras picked up anything?"

Joseph nodded. "They should have. Let me call Nathaniel and get him to pull the videos." Having made the call, he turned to Matt. "Now, are you ready to believe me, that you're a target?"

Matt stared out the front window. "I am, but why?" He sighed. "We're not finding out now. On to Sarah's, James."

Joseph threw him a disgusted look. "It's Joseph, and I am NOT your chauffeur."

Joseph studied the area around Sarah's house as they walked up to it. A slight movement next door caught his eye. "I'll be right back. I just want to check something."

Matt gave him a questioning look and then shrugged. After what they just went through, Joseph was jumpy. He rang Sarah's door bell, thinking back to a few nights ago. He was just so glad she wasn't hurt.

There was movement at the window and then the door opened. Sarah stood there, glaring at him. "What are you doing here? You're not supposed to be driving."

He held up his hands as he grinned at her. "I didn't. Joseph did."

She peered around him. "If he did, where is he?"

"He went to check out something at Doug's."

Sarah stared at him, then spun heading for the back door. Matt reached for her arm and stopped her.

"No, let him check it out. We had an incident on the way in, and he's jumpy." At her look, he continued, "We had a car that looked at if it was going to ram us. Same colour of car as the other night."

Her face paling. Sarah reached to steady herself on the wall. "What is going on?"

He shook his head as Joseph tapped at the front door and then entered. He had a grim look on his face that Matt didn't like.

"Sarah, we need you to pack some things and come with us."

She stood, hands on hips, and glared at him. "Just like that, pack some things and come with you. No explanation. Just orders. I don't think so." She turned and stormed away.

"You handled that well, Joseph. What did you find?"

The grim look tightened on Joseph's face and a hard look came into his eyes. "Someone was standing at the back of Doug's yard, watching Sarah's place. He's been there for a while too."

Matt's head whipped around to stare at the kitchen and then back at Joseph. "She is a target."

"You both are, and we need to find out why. I've called Abe, and he was calling Caleb. Abe wants both of you back at Rebel's."

"He can want that all he wants, but it's not going to be that easy to convince Sarah to come."

"Joseph, did you say he had been there for a while?" Sarah's voice was barely a whisper. At his nod, her eyes closed. "I have had some things moved around outside the house, and I couldn't figure out who was doing it. They can't get in, I have too good an alarm system." Her eyes open, she looked first at Joseph, then at Matt. "Is Matt a target because of me?"

"We don't know, Sarah. We just haven't figured it out." Joseph stopped, knowing the next words would not be taken well. "We need to trace back to your accident and beyond that. Caleb is already going back over everything. We need to know what you remember."

Sarah was shaking her head. "I can't. I just can't."

"Sarah, in order to help you, and to keep both you and Matt alive, we need to know what you know or what your impressions are."

She turned away from the men, arms wrapped around her waist. She started to shake, knowing that she now had to face the past, to unearth what she had buried deep enough she thought never to see it again. She jerked at Matt's hands came to her shoulders and turning her towards him, pulled her into his hug. She stood for a moment, then stepped back, meeting the puzzled look in his eyes.

She spoke, not taking her eyes off Matt. "If I go, Joseph, I need to be able to come and go. I have contracts that we need to fulfill."

Joseph nodded. "We can work around that. I'm sure Abe will agree that we can be yours and Matt's security team for now."

Matt turned his head to glare at him, meeting his innocent look.

Sarah turned and walked to her bedroom, saying over her shoulder, "Miss Muffet and Spider have to come too. I'm not leaving them."

"Miss Muffet? Spider?" Joseph mouthed, then looked around.

Matt starting laughing. "Her cats. Come on. We'll need to round them up as well as their supplies.

Caleb stood on Doug's back deck, studying his yard, and then Sarah's. "He was standing whereabouts?"

Eddie pointed to where Joseph had found the tracks. "He had a direct line of sight to her house from there. He would have been hidden at night too, if Doug had been home."

"So, who is he after? He tries to run them down, stalks Sarah, tries to run Joseph and Matt of the road today?"

Eddie shook his head. "I have no idea. All I can say is, here we go again." He sounded grumpy. He just knew what was coming up and he didn't like it.

Caleb shook his head. "I know. My thoughts too. And before you ask, no, Hannah doesn't have a name yet."

Abe watched from the office building as Matt

and Joseph helped Sarah move into the closest cottage. The cottages had been used in years past when his father and uncle had run a vacation site for VIPs. He and Rebecca had decided against continuing that. Now he was glad he had the cottages to offer one to Sarah. He walked towards them, listening to Matt and Joseph discuss her pets.

Abe stopped and peered into the carriers, then at the cottage. "If you leave them in their carriers for a bit, they'll get used to the place."

Matt glared at him. "I know that. I just don't know if Sarah will."

"She will. She knows that." Abe looked past Matt at Joseph and caught the negative shake of his head. He sighed. No, Sarah was not going to make it easy for him to get the information Caleb needed.

Abe stopped beside Sarah as she stood looking around the cottage. "I don't like this, Abe."

"I know you don't. The other option would be for Caleb to put you under 24-hour guard, and you would like that even less."

She glared at him, then stomped across the room to pull out the cats' supplies. "That would be horrible." She stopped, then turned to him. "I'm sorry. I wasn't nice. I just don't like not being in my own home."

"No, you don't. It's your security blanket, where you feel safe. You don't know this place and don't know if you will be safe." She looked at him, head tilted to one side as he continued, "We will do our best to keep you safe. One of my guys will be with you at all times on your job site and wherever else you need to be." He held up his hand. "It won't be Matt on his own. If he's with you, someone else will be too."

She sank down into one of the chairs. "Thanks, Abe. With John away, I can't be off the job. I'll be having to move around between sites and the office. I'll also need to be going places to do estimates. Most of the estimates Clark does now, but there are times when John or I have to be the one."

He nodded. "I get that. We'll manage." He stopped and stared at the door. "Before they come in with your cats, which by the way I love the names for, both Caleb and I need to know what is going on, what happened in the past. I know you don't want to talk about it, but at some time, you'll have to. There are a couple of days coming up with the team will have to be away because of scheduling. Caleb will pick up your security and Gideon is willing to step in. I suspect Rebecca will be down here a lot, having another female around here has been her wish for a long time." He paused. "Just remember, Sarah, God is still in control. Sometimes He draws us aside for a time, to get our attention, to let us heal, to help us work through things. We don't often like the way He does that. I don't need to tell you that. You've already been there and done that. Guess He decided you needed a refresher course."

"I could do without the refresher course, thank you very much, but you're right. That's what He does." She stopped and stared as the lights flickered. "Can you get me a really good flashlight, Caleb? And a ladder. You've got something going on with your electricity here."

He looked at her, then the lights. "Sure. I'll be right back."

The three men watched as Sarah pulled herself through the attic hatch. She shone her light around and then they could hear her moving around above them. Her voice came back down.

"Abe. I need you up here. Just be very careful where you're moving. I have something I need to show you."

The three men exchanged glances, and then Abe levered himself through the hatch. The two men below could hear muted conversation but couldn't pick up the words.

"Joseph, go get Paul, will you?"

Joseph was gone before he had completely finished. Abe came back down the ladder as Paul entered. Abe nodded at the hatch. "I need you to look at something Sarah's found."

Paul came back down the ladder and Sarah followed, pulling the hatch closed as she came. "I don't see any other electrical issues, Abe, other than what I showed you. I would suggest we check all the other cottages soon."

Abe nodded, his attention on Paul. "Is that what we think it is?"

Paul nodded. "It is. It's fairly recent too by the looks of it." He help up a small listening device. "I don't think it's been run to any cameras but we'll look around to be sure. Sorry, Sarah, this is not how we wanted to welcome you to Rebel's."

She shrugged. "It goes with the territory. It's

not the first time I've found things like that hidden away."

They stared at her, and she looked up. "It's true. Ask John. He's found them too."

Abe studied her, then the device in Paul's hand. "Sarah, I'm going to ask you something, and I want you to think very hard about it. Where have you found these and would this have had something to do with your accident two years ago?"

She started to shake her head, then stopped. Her face whitened. Matt caught her as her knees buckled and helped her to a chair. Raising a shaking hand to her mouth, she stared at Paul's hand, then looked up at Abe. She nodded. "It may well be connected. I never thought of it before. I gave the device to John and he turned it over to the police. I'm not sure now who it was, but he would remember."

Abe nodded, a grim look on his face. "I'll speak with Eddie or Caleb and give John a call. For now, we know this cottage is safe, thanks to you. We'll have to check all the others today."

Matt stayed with her as the other men left. He wandered into the kitchen, opening cabinet doors. She smelled the aroma of fresh brewed coffee and then turned to the cat carriers, letting her two cats out to wander around. Spider wove around her feet, and she picked her up and cuddled her close. Sarah turned to look around the room, not feeling quite as secure as she had earlier. She sank down on the brown leather couch and kicked off her shoes. Her hip was starting to act up and she knew it was from the tension coursing through her body.

Matt handed her a cup of coffee, then sat down on the other end of the couch. "It doesn't make it easier, does it?"

"What doesn't?"

"Finding that. It just adds to who and what."

She looked at him. "It can't be me this time. No one knew I was coming until about an hour ago and they wouldn't have been able to get in here in daylight and plant that."

Matt turned his mug in his hands, not sure how to continue. "Do you ever blame God for what happened to you, Sarah? It changed your life drastically."

She turned her head to look at him, then set her cup down on the coffee table. Spider crawled up on the back of the couch and cuddled close to her neck, and she reached to stroke her back. "No, I never did. I don't know why, but that never crossed my mind. It could have, I guess. I could have asked "Why me" but then I was taught that God allows good and bad to even believers. The correct question would be "Why not me". I will likely never know who did it or the reason why. That's not what I am to focus on. God knows who and why. It's His to avenge, not mine. I need to keep my focus on Him and allow Him to heal me and allow Him to work on my heart to forgive whoever it was."

Matt sat with his eyes closed, listening to her. She was right. He had work to do on his own healing and forgiveness. As someone who worked in the medical field as well as the security field, he knew this. "Thank you, Sarah."

"For what?"

"For your wisdom. You have explained something to me in a way that no one ever has before. I can see where you get your peace." He stood. "I'll let you get settled. For our meals, we quite often eat together with Abe, Gideon and Rebecca. You're welcome to join us. I suspect Rebecca will be down here shortly to invite you herself."

She watched as he walked away, head down. Her heart cried out to God to work in his life and heal him from whatever was in the past.

****

He stood once again in the shadows across from her house. He had not seen her all day, so where was she? That man from the security team had almost got him but he was too quick. He would track her down and find what it was she had. He turned to study Doug's house, where he could see movement against the light. An idea was fermenting but it would be a last resort he knew.

Chapter 6

Murphy studied the area around John's shop and shook his head. He didn't like it. It just wouldn't be easy to keep secure, even though it was fenced. He walked through to the shop, studying the entries and the windows, then shook his head again. John had good security but it could be better. He went to find Sarah.

Listening to her as she went over the work orders with the other three electricians, he could understand why she wanted to be there. She was good at her job, good at delegating. She finally turned and came towards him, the limp evident.

"So, I know you don't like the security. I can see it in your face." Sarah grinned at him.

"It's good but it could be better. Does Matt know you do that?"

"Do what?"

"Read minds," he joked, then turned serious. "Sarah, there are some things I would recommend to improve your security here. If you want, I can go over them with you or go over them with John.

"Go over them with John, he sets that all up. Remind me to give you his number and email." She turned to head into the office. "I need to take care of some stuff here, I'll be a couple of hours, then I have to head out to the job sites."

Murphy nodded. "That's fine. I have some research I need to do any way."

"The break room's that way. Help yourself to the coffee. I think Clark brought in some goodies this morning, his wife usually sends something."

Murphy went looking for Sarah a couple of hours later, finding her immersed in paperwork, building plans spread around her. He handed her a cup of coffee, knowing she hadn't had one in a while.

"Thanks." She took it absentmindedly and sipped. "This is good. I vote you make our coffee all the time."

Murphy laughed, then nodded at the paperwork. "It looks as if you're going to be a while longer."

She shook her head and looked at her watch. "No, only about 15 minutes. It always looks worse than it is."

Murphy dropped into a chair near her, his own cup of coffee in his hand, and watched as she searched through manuals and made notes. Fifteen minutes later, she was rolling up the plans and stacking the files neatly on the table in the office. She turned to him and smiled. "Bored already?"

He shook his head. "No. I've just never been this close to watching how a trade works. It's different from what I do."

She searched his face. "That it is. I need to drop off some permit applications at city hall and then head out to the job sites. Are you sure you're okay with this?"

Murphy watched the conflicting emotions

crossing her face. "I am, Sarah. It's what I do for a living, security. There are times when it can really intense but most of the time it's like this." He hesitated to speak, knowing she was not going to like the restrictions he would be placing on her. "We need to go over some things, Sarah. And I already know you won't like them."

"That bad, eh?" She laughed at him. "Murphy, it's okay, really. I know there will be restrictions. There has to be. And no, I won't like them. I've been through enough in my life to know that bad happens and because it does, my life changes."

"I wish everyone was so agreeable as you." Murphy waited while she picked up the paperwork she needed and then followed her through to the back door. He stopped her as she went to open it and step through. "This is one of the things you won't like. When we're with you, you no longer go through the door first. You let us."

She tried to stare him down but lost the contest. "All right," she sighed, "go, do your job."

Murphy gave her a half smile and then ducked out the door. He was back in a few minutes. "Looks clear. So which vehicle are we taking?"

"Yours. I don't need equipment today and I want to get Clark to lock my vehicle in the shop."

"Give me your keys and I'll do it now."

She handed him her keys and watched as he walked towards her van. She heard the beep of the key fob and then the van disappeared in a ball of flames. Murphy went flying backwards, landing awkwardly and then lying still. Sarah screamed, then scrambling for her phone, she ran towards Murphy. He was starting to move as she reached him.

"Murphy!" She couldn't get his attention and was starting to panic. She could hear the sirens approaching and looked up. Movement to the front of the yard stopped her gaze and she stared at the figure standing there, hoodie raised to conceal the face.

Murphy grasped her arm and pulled her away from the fire, grimacing with pain as he moved, and then shoving her into his vehicle. He stood beside it, eyes scanning the area.

Caleb approached them as the firefighters were wrapping up their hoses.

"What happened, Murphy?"

Murphy's face with grim and tense. "Someone tried to get to her. If we had taken her vehicle, she could be dead by now. Whatever it was, I triggered it with the key fob. If Sarah had been alone, she likely would have been a lot closer to the vehicle than I was. Women wait until they're close to their vehicles to unlock the doors."

Caleb ducked his head so he could watch Sarah through the window. She stared at the spot her van had been parked in. the van now just a blackened mass of twisted metal. Her face was white and tense. He could see the fear in her face, something he didn't think he had ever seen or ever expected to see.

"I'll have our guys take a look at it, but they'll not likely find much."

Murphy shook his head. "Not likely, but I can tell you it was connected to the locks and set off by the key fob. Unless….." He spun to study the area, searching the faces of the onlookers, trying to find one that stood out.

Sarah popped her door open. "Murphy, there was someone here. I saw him before you moved us back from the fire." Terror shook her voice.

"Where?" Murphy turned to stare at where she pointed. There was no one there now. "I'll be right back."

Murphy jogged back across the lot, dodging the remaining firefighters. "He's not there now and I don't see anything that showed he was." As Sarah opened her mouth, he held up his hand. "I believe you, Sarah. We're going to want to get your statement about that. Caleb will do it for you or have one of his people do it."

Caleb nodded. Whatever was going on just got bigger and more dangerous. He turned as he heard someone calling Sarah's name. He recognized the man and waved him through the lines. Sarah was out of the SUV before they could stop her and hugging the man.

"John, when did you get back?"

"Just now. Meg's grandmother's better and she sent me home." He looked at the mess in their yard and sighed. "Looks like I'm in time. What have you been doing?"

She shook her head as she turned to look around. "Not me, buddy, not me. Come on, I have to stay with Murphy and he's not happy with me right now."

John looked down at her and then at the two men standing by the vehicle. No, Sarah, they're not happy with you. And I'm not either.

"John." Caleb reached to shake his head. "I didn't expect you back yet. Emily's better?"

"She is. Meg and her mom are staying for a few more days, then driving home. She sent me back." His eyes took in the activity. "It looks as if I'm just in time."

"You are. Clark was here just after we arrived. I sent him back to the job. He's a hard man to convince."

"He is. He takes his work very seriously." His eyes were sending a message to Caleb and Caleb nodded. Clark was looking out for Sarah without her knowing it.

"Murphy." John reached to shake his hand. "I'm not sure why you're here but I understand you got caught in the action."

"I did." Murphy's eyes were still studying the remaining onlookers. "I suggest we move our meeting to somewhere indoors."

Caleb spoke up. "I agree. I need to talk to you two any way. How be we meet at the office?"

Sarah shook her head. "Absolutely not. If you want to talk to me, you'll find me at Abe's. Murphy, let's go."

"I would, except my vehicle is still blocked in."

She turned in frustration, then was walking off before any of the three men could stop her. She disappeared into the crowd. Murphy looked at the other two in disbelief, and then ran after her.

John laughed. "He's got his hands full

protecting her.”

Caleb nodded. “He does and she needs to realize she has to let them.” He paused, then looked over at John. “Has she ever talked to you about her accident years ago?”

John thought about that, then shook his head. “I don’t think she’s talked to anyone about it much. Do you think it’s related?”

“It’s one thing we’re running through. At this point, we looking at events and people known to both Matt and Sarah.”

Murphy came up beside them. “I can’t believe I lost her. She was gone before I could even get to the street.”

Caleb nodded. “She did this once before, after her accident. Her Dad knew where to go and find her but neither one said where it was.” He sighed. “We’ll have to let her come back on her own, unless we find out where she is.”

John agreed. “When she gets this stubborn, and I’ve only seen in once in a while, you just step back. Speaking of which, she had a folder in her hand when she left.”

Murphy looked in the front seat. “We were heading for city hall to drop off some paperwork, permit applications I think she said.”

John had his phone out and was speaking to someone. “Amy, have you seen Sarah today? I’ve been trying to reach her.”

“No but Beth said something about meeting her. She’s not back yet.”

"Can you have Beth call me? It's important that I speak with Sarah today." As he hung up, he shook his head. "She hasn't been there but she's meeting Beth and chances are she'll hand off the paperwork to her. Sarah always has everything ready to go, cheques and all."

Caleb ran his hand through his hair in frustration, then walked over to speak with the fire chief. Watching the other two men, he still couldn't believe that Sarah had just walked away from them like she did, but then again he could understand her frustration.

As he walked back to the group, his phone rang. It was Eddie.

"Eddie, what's up?"

"Did you lose someone, Caleb?" Eddie's voice was amused.

Caleb steps slowed and then he stopped walking. "She's with you?"

"She is. She doesn't want me to tell you where she is, but I will. There's a condition though, or she'll run again and then no one will find her. She's adamant about that."

Caleb moved to where the other men were standing and looking up, saw Matt and Joseph headed his way. Great, it just got so much better. Then, sorry, Lord, I'm just frustrated. I know You're handling it but if You let me know some of it, that would be great.

Matt looked around. "Where is she?"

The men shared a glance, then turned to Caleb

as he closed his phone. "I know where she is but Eddie says she's adamant about what she wants done. If we don't do what she's asking, she'll run again and this time, Eddie says no one will find her."

Matt glared at him. "And you agreed?"

Caleb stared him down until Matt dropped his eyes. "I did. I know Sarah, as does Eddie and John. If she says she'll run and we won't find her, then that's what will happen. Not even Doug would be able to find her and those two have been as close as brother and sister over the years. I'm not even sure if her father would know where she would run to. You can bet she's got places picked out all over town."

Matt drew a deep breath. "So where is she and how do we proceed?"

Caleb studied the men watching him and then turned to look at the remnants of the van. "Matt, did you notice anything the morning you all had breakfast?"

Matt narrowed his eyes as he thought back. "I did. I saw a man walking away from where her van was parked and looking at something in his hand. No. You don't think….." His voice trailed away.

"It's possible he's the one. She told Eddie she felt like she was being watched and has been for a while. What her 'a while' is, Eddie didn't say and I'm not sure she even told him. This is what we're doing. I'm taking you and Murphy to meet her. Once we can get you two to a place we can keep you safe, Abe is going to move in with your team. He's passed off the assignment you were to go on this week and gladly did it."

Eddie met them in the parking lot of the cafe. He was leaning against his vehicle, studying something in his hand. He looked up as Caleb walked towards him. Matt and Murphy had stayed in Caleb's car.

"Eddie."

"Caleb." Eddie looked at Caleb. "She's hurting, Caleb. I haven't seen her hurt like this before. It's worse than when she had her accident and was left for dead. Her faith is shaken and that takes a lot for that to happen with her. She's not sure God even cares about her any more."

"Has she said anything at all?"

Eddie shook his head. "No, she hasn't. That's not surprising. She said to give you this." Eddie handed over the paper he held. "She wanted you to wait until dark, but I told her that wasn't happening. I was prepared to arrest her as being a material witness to the fire if she fought me, and she knew that."

"Thanks, Eddie. How's the investigation coming on her accident?"

"Now, that's an interesting question. I'm finding our department did a very poor job on that investigation. Lots of stuff got swept aside or left out."

Caleb's hand stilled as he was tucking the note into his pocket. "Are you serious? I don't like that. Is the officer still on the force?"

Eddie shook his head. "No, he's not. He was killed in that deep water diving accident about four months after that. I wonder if it really was an accident."

"Keep digging, Eddie. Bring Frankie in to help."

Caleb returned to his vehicle and dug the note out of his pocket, reading the address. He shook his head. She was good, he thought, really good. Who would ever have thought to find her there?

"Where is she?" Matt's quiet voice broke the silence.

Caleb studied the note, then handed it to Murphy seated beside him.

"She's there?"

"Looks like it."

"Where?" Matt demanded from the back seat.

Murphy and Caleb exchanged a glance, then Murphy spoke. "She is in an apartment down town, near the police department. No one would know that as it's not in her name."

"An apartment."

Caleb nodded. "An apartment. I don't know why or how, but she does. She's also very particular about how we go there. So you're going to do exactly what I say, both of you, or I go alone. Got it?"

****

He knew she had seen him but he didn't think she would recognize him, it had been so long. He watched her house but she hadn't come back. So where was she? He needed to reach her but if she kept hiding, how was he to do that? Following the men guarding her didn't work. They almost had him the other day. He wasn't used to the tricks they used. But who had blown up her van? It wasn't him, so who was it?

Chapter 7

Caleb tapped at the apartment door and waited for Sarah to answer. Matt and Murphy stood beside him. Caleb was not sure how Sarah would react to Matt being there, but he wanted the two of them together. He needed them together. Until they could figure out who was the target and why, they were going nowhere alone.

He heard a chain on the door and then the door opened slowly. He stepped through, followed by Matt and Murphy. Sarah closed and locked the door behind them and then motioned to the couches.

Matt studied the apartment. It wasn't Sarah's, he could tell, the style wasn't hers. So, whose was it? He turned to look at her, and his heart broke at the devastation he saw there.

Sarah refused to sit, instead pacing the area between the couches and the kitchen, her limp evident. She seemed to be trying to make up her mind to say something, but then her head would shake and she would resume pacing. Caleb and Murphy sat and waited patiently, knowing Sarah would speak when she was ready. She turned and came and stood in front of Matt.

"I'm sorry, Matt, that I wasn't there when you got there, but I'm not sorry I ran. I'm also sorry that Eddie saw me. I wouldn't be here if he hadn't." She spoke over her shoulder to Caleb, her eyes still fixed on Matt, an inscrutable look in them. "You asked me about my accident, Caleb, and anything around that time I could remember. I've kept quiet for years as it involves another person, but I learned today that person is dead. So here goes."

She turned and dropped down onto the couch by Matt, staring at Caleb. "You're not going to like it. You had a dirty cop at the time, and he was bought off to run me down. I still haven't figured out exactly who, but I wasn't the first one he helped to have an "accident". I know of at least five others something similar happened to. Four of them are dead, that's how deadly their "accidents" were. The fifth one left town and hasn't been back."

Caleb nodded. "Eddie and I had come to that conclusion. He pulled the investigative report for your accident. It held a lot of missing information. The officer you mentioned, he died in a deep water diving accident about four or five months after yours."

Sarah snorted. "Accident, my foot. He was killed to keep him quiet."

Murphy studied her, then a movement by Matt caught his attention. Something was going on there, he thought, and it's related to his past.

Sarah gave Caleb all the information she could remember, as well as impressions she had formed. He knew they didn't have a lot to go on but they had worked with less before. "I want to bring Gideon in on this, in an official capacity. He has resources that I wish we could use but we can't."

Sarah nodded, fatigue now evident in her face. "I understand. Now what, Caleb? You know my story, you must know Matt's. So which one of us is he after?"

"That we don't know yet. It's almost as if there are two of them, and one of them is determined to hurt either one of you, it doesn't matter who. It's like he's thinking that if he hurts one of you, he hurts the other."

Matt spoke up. "That's what I don't understand. Sarah says stuff has been going on for a while, but we only just meet. So how does that work?"

Caleb shook his head. "That's what we'll be delving into. Anything with your past that you can remember, any threats from around here or your home area, you need to let me know."

Sarah stood and headed for the door. "If that's all you've got, I'm gone."

Matt was at the door before she could reach it. He refused to let her leave. The other two men watched, somewhat amused, at the contest going on between the two. Sarah finally sighed, took a couple of steps away and stopped. Matt, relieved, moved away from the door and back towards his seat. None of them expected what happened next. Sarah was at the door, unlocked it and was gone before they even realized what she was up to. Matt dashed after but there was no sign of her. He stood in the hallway, trying to hear footsteps but couldn't hear any.

Caleb and Murphy appeared from either end of the hall, shaking their heads. They hadn't found her either. Caleb searched the apartment for any clue and then left, telling them he'd be back shortly. Murphy headed back into the apartment as well, phone in hand to brief Abe on what was going on. It was getting strange, he thought, where she went. Matt hadn't followed him, and he stepped back out the door. No Matt. Now, where had he gone?

Matt stood inside the neighbouring apartment, Sarah in his arms, her hand against his mouth. She was listening to the noise in the hallway. Finally, she moved away from him.

"Sarah, what is going on? Why did you run?" Matt's frustration was evident.

"It's okay. Caleb knows. Eddie told him."

"What do you mean, Caleb knows?"

"Eddie knew I was running and came up with a plan. He let Caleb know. We want to keep it as quiet as we can so we can figure out who and what."

"Sarah, that's not fair to my team, and you know it. They're putting their lives on the line to keep us alive."

She nodded. "I know. Eddie was headed out to talk to Abe. Murphy likely knows what the plan is now too."

"That's what I want to know, what it the plan?"

A tap at the door stopped the conversation. Matt stepped over and looked through the peephole, then opening the door, stepped back to let Murphy in. He could tell Murphy was highly displeased, almost angry.

"I don't like this, Sarah. You knew we were

keeping you safe and you pull this stunt.”

Sarah stared back at him, not giving an inch. “I know, but it’s my life, not yours, that’s really on the line. Now, we have to move and if you two don’t want to come, then stay here.”

She moved towards the door but Murphy’s hand stopped her. She stood, not looking at him, waiting for him to speak.

“Sarah, I know it’s your life. We’re all well aware of that. But this time it involves someone else. Matt. And unless I miss my guess, you’ve become important to him.” He stopped but she refused to speak. “You need to let us do our job. It’s what we do—security.”

She shrugged his hand from her arm and opened the door. “He’s too close, Murphy, he was at the fire. He’s been around my house. He may well have been the one doing the sabotage on the sites I’ve been working at. Where was your team then?” She turned to stare at him, eyes glinting with anger and some other emotion Murphy couldn’t read. “If he’s the one responsible for my accident, then he tore something away from me I’ll never get back. He also had other people killed. Where was your team then? It doesn’t matter that I have law enforcement people in my life. He just doesn’t care.”

She turned and walked through the door. Matt and Murphy exchanged a glance then went after her. This time she was waiting for them. Murphy led them down the two flights of stairs and then motioned for them to wait. He was back in a minute and sending them to the vehicle Eddie had left waiting for them. Murphy slid behind the wheel and headed away from the down town area.

He drove straight for the highway and headed south, then after about 10 miles turned onto a secondary road. It would have been a pretty drive, Sarah thought, but for the reason they were here. Farms dotted the area, with groves of old growth trees sprinkled here and there. She could see the cattle and horses in the fields and the odd field of sheep. She had suspicions as to where they were headed and didn't like it. Why did you choose this place, Caleb? You know the history of it.

Murphy slowed and turned onto a narrower one-lane road. He hoped he didn't meet any traffic coming his way, there wasn't much room to pass. He breathed a sigh of relief as he found the lane he was looking for and turned it. As he moved his head, he caught the look on Sarah's face. Now what brought that on, he wondered? She's not happy with this choice. Caleb and Abe, what did you do?e.

Sarah sank down onto the chair with relief. She was exhausted, tired, and felt filthy. She just wanted to find her bed and collapse on it for the night but she wasn't sure if she would even be allowed that luxury yet. She laid her head back and close her eyes, the sounds around her fading as she drifted off. Matt grabbed a blanket from the cupboard and gently covered her.

Murphy watched, then nodded. Abe was right. Matt's feelings for Sarah were there in the little things, even though he may not have said anything to her yet.

Matt turned to the Murphy. "We're secure here?"

"About as secure as we can get. This guy is good though. I'd like to know who he is."

"There's more than one of them, and I don't think they're working together, at least not yet."

Murphy stopped with the coffee carafe in his hand. He was just making coffee. "Why do you say that?"

"Two targets, two different people, two different lifestyles, two different home towns. Two victims. Two villains."

"I agree." Murphy studied the wall across from where he was standing taking note of the calendar hanging there that was from five years ago. "It's just too bizarre to think one person was after you. Caleb will be calling shortly. He's wanting to get Sarah's statement."

"It won't be tonight, Murphy. She's asleep and needs it. Short of it being life or death, I'm not waking her up." Matt stood and moved back to watch Sarah. "Which is her bedroom?"

"This way." Murphy watched at Matt scooped Sarah up and carried her through to the room they had assigned her to. Closing the door, Matt headed back to the kitchen.

The dark form stood over Murphy and chuckled in glee. He had taken out the security man on his own. Now he could get to Sarah. There was only the one man left, and if he threatened him, she would do what he wanted, he was sure. He tugged at his hoodie to make sure it was secure, slipped on the sunglasses and then headed for the house. He opened the door and listened in the early morning sunlight. No noise.

He crept down the hall, listening at doorways. He stepped back into an empty room as one of the doors opened and Matt stepped out. Matt hesitated as he stepped into the hall, sensing something was wrong. Waiting until he had passed him, the man came at Matt from behind, looping an arm around his neck and pushing the weapon into his side, the floor creaking beneath his feet.

"Do want I want, and you'll live. She will too."

Matt was startled, but his training kicked in. Go along, he thought, go along until you have a chance to act. Please, God, let it be soon. Keep Sarah safe. He was pulled around and shoved towards Sarah's room.

"Get her up." He was ordered.

He knocked at her door and called her name. Hearing no answer, the weapon was driven deeper into his side. He knocked again and this time he heard Sarah moving towards the door. She opened it and stopped, fear showing on her face as she took in the two in front on her.

"Move," she was ordered, "move out the front of the house. Any noise or any tricks, he dies."

Sarah watched Matt and saw him nod. She moved past him and out of the house. Where were Muprhy? She was afraid, not afraid for her, but afraid for her friend. She knew Matt would be searching for him as well. They were forced down the lane and then into an older truck, Matt behind the wheel, with Sarah in the middle. The weapon was driven into her side with force, and she gasped. Matt turned and saw the eyes staring at him faintly through the dark glasses. He turned back and started up the truck, following the directions he was given. Where were they being taken and who by?

Murphy stirred, his hand going to his head. He tried to drag himself up, to get to Sarah and Matt, but collapsed back into darkness.

Caleb and Abe stood at the open door of the cabin. One look at each other and with weapons drawn, they entered and searched. There was no one around.

Abe's eyes met Caleb's. Something was so wrong! Matt and Sarah should be here in the cabin, along with one of Abe's men. They cautiously made their way out of the cabin, searching as they went.

"Over here, Abe." Caleb knelt by Murphy and felt for a pulse. He was alive. Caleb gently turned his head and winced at the blood he could see that had dried on the back of it.

"Murphy?"

Caleb nodded. "Someone got to him."

Hours later, Eddie stood in the conference room, flanked by Frankie, and stared at Caleb. "Just like that, they're gone, and Murphy was down? Why is it, every time we stash someone away in a safe house, it's compromised and we have to move them, or they disappear on their own or with help? Who's giving us away?"

"I don't know, Eddie, and I wish I did. No one knew about this place until I told Abe and I told him in person. So how did word get out?"

Frankie listened to the two friends, and caught the undertone of anger in both their voices, not at one another but at the situation. God, we could sure use some help here right about now. Please keep them safe. Give us the wisdom we are going to need to find them.

"Caleb, Eddie, please." Frankie's voice cut through and got their attention. "Where do we start?"

Caleb turned and stared across his office. "That's the problem. We don't know where to start. We have no idea who we're looking for or why. It could be either one of them. John's going back over the sabotage on the job sites to see if he can find anything. He's also pulling records for where they found those listening devices. Once he gets them to us, we'll have someone start following them up."

Eddie spoke. "What about Matt? I know Abe did a really through background search on him, like he does all his men. Did he find anything?"

"No, other than the accident that claimed the lives of Matt's dad, brother and sister." Caleb turned to Eddie. "Now, that's somewhere we can start. Matt mentioned that the driver lost a lot and his family was very angry with Matt and his mother. We need to look into that more."

****

He had missed them, somehow. Someone else had them. He stood in the shadows of the trees, sunlight flickering across his face, and watched at the cabin area was searched. He knew they wouldn't find anything; this guy was too good.

Chapter 8

att pulled the truck to a stop in the out-of-the way campground and turned it off. He waited, not sure for what. The man searched the area around them, then pulling Sarah out of his door, motioned for Matt to get out as well. Matt slowly rounded the vehicle to stand by Sarah, her hand seeking his. They watched and waited, for what they didn't know. The man paced back and forth in front of them, growing more agitated by the moment. Pulling out his phone as he felt it vibrate, he listened, and then turned to stare at them, eyes narrowing in menace. Sticking his phone away, he pointed his weapon at Sarah.

"Move down that pathway behind you. No tricks or she's dead."

Matt and Sarah shared a glance, and then Matt turned to study the path behind them. His heart sank. It led towards the forest and he knew it then led into another county once they had crossed the ridge. How were they to get away? A shove from behind started him on his way, Sarah's hand clapped tight in his. Where were they headed?

Sarah's steps were lagging. She just couldn't walk any more. Matt had tried to help her but he know she needed to rest. He stopped, eyes searching for somewhere she could rest. He felt a shove from behind and spun. The weapon was inches from his face.

"Go ahead. Shoot me. But she needs to rest. She can't keep walking like you're pushing us." Matt glared at the man, eyes hard and angry. Somehow he had to take care of Sarah and find some way to get her away from this man. God, he prayed, I could use some help about now. What do you want me to do? *Wait,* he heard whispered to him, *wait. I have a purpose for this. Trust me.*

Matt looked around, convinced someone was standing beside him. He shook his head, and then turned his attention back to the man holding them captive.

"Sarah, we're stopping here so you can rest. There's an area just over there where you can lean against that stump. Do you need help?" He caught her negative head shake as she moved to sit.

Matt was right, she needed to sit. And just maybe it would give Matt a chance to come up with a plan to get them away. She leaned her head back and closed her eyes. She hurt all over and her heart hurt too. She prayed that Abe's men were alive and unharmed. She opened her eyes just enough to see and watched at Matt faced down their captor. Please, Matt, don't do something foolish. I need you. You need to stay alive.

Matt turned his back on their captor to study the area around him. He could hear the man moving restlessly, knowing he didn't like the fact Sarah had had to rest. His eyes narrowing, he searched for a way out, but something held him back from trying to escape. Had it been that word from God that did it, or was it knowing Sarah would never be able to make a run for it? His gaze turned to Sarah and found her watching him. She nodded, letting him know she was ready to move forward. As he reached to help her up, a blow on his arm stopped him. He spun and found the weapon inches from his face. He froze, knowing one wrong move would be his last. Sarah rose and caught his hand.

"Where do you want us to go now?" She asked. "Which way?"

The man stood, arm extended, weapon pointed at Matt's head. "Go forward. No more stops. No more rest."

Matt turned and walked forward, pacing his steps to make it easier for Sarah. He prayed the man didn't catch on. Sarah's hand tightened on his and he knew she understood. Soon they were in a clearing and ordered to stop. Matt rested his arm around Sarah to help her balance. He studied the area, looking for a way out for them. He watched as the man paced. His eyes narrowed as he watched. He felt as if he knew him but he wasn't sure. Why did he look familiar?

Sarah tugged at his sleeve and he looked down. She glanced at the man and then pointed towards the trees. Frowning, his eyes followed her finger and then his face relaxed. There just might be a way out, if they could distract the man. Then he heard the voice again, telling him to wait. He shook his head at Sarah, then let his eyes move past her to where the man was standing, watching them. If they had made even the slightly move, they would have been dead.

"Come here." The man's voice brooked no refusal. They walked towards him, across the few feet of forest floor that separated them, scuffing through the fallen leaves and twigs. They stopped just outside his read.

"Turn around."

Matt stared at the man, trying to get a sense of what was going on. He's good, Matt thought. He doesn't let anything show.

"Turn around, or she dies." The weapon was pointed at Sarah.

They turned, not knowing what was coming. Matt's hands were jerked roughly behind him and bound. Then he was shoved across the glade and to the ground. He fell awkwardly, then straightened himself up to a sitting position, eyes searching for Sarah. She stood where he had left her, hands on her mouth, and fear in her very stance. He stared, trying to convey calmness to her, but he didn't know if she would understand what he was trying to say to her. Sarah was pulled to the opposite side of the glade and shoved to the ground. Matt heard the muted cry she gave as she landed on her bad hip. She wasn't bound, but their captor stood close. Every few minutes, he pulled out his phone and searched it, then looked at the sky. Night was closing in and they had no shelter.

Abe looked up as Murphy dropped into a seat in his office. The bruise on his temple had spread, giving him a black eye.

"Your head still hurting?"

Murphy glared at him. "Of course it is. And don't ask me to shake it, because I won't. It will fall off if I do."

Abe smiled at Murphy's testiness, knowing it

wasn't directed at him. "We can't have that, now can we?" He sobered. "Seriously, Murphy, how are you feeling?"

"I'm ticked off, is what I am. How did he get by me? He got to Matt through Sarah."

Abe nodded as he studied Murphy. "That's what I'm thinking too. How did he do it? It makes me think that this guy is after Matt, not Sarah, and is using her to threaten him. But who could it be?"

"I've been going back over our assignments since Matt joined us. I've come up with a few names." Murphy pulled out a sheet of paper from his shirt pocket and handed it over to Abe.

Abe unfolded it and started reading. As he got to the second-to-last name, his eyes froze. His face grew grim. He laid the paper down on his desk, and with a faraway look in his eyes, contemplated the name. He tapped the paper, and brought his focus to Murphy. "This one, Murphy; the second-to-last one. I remember it. He took such a dislike to Matt, I had to move Matt to a different position on the team for that assignment. If I hadn't needed him, I would have asked him to come home, which wouldn't have been fair to him."

Murphy nodded. "I agree. We'll need to get this to Caleb."

Abe nodded, then looked at his watch. "I'm to meet with Caleb at the department in about 30 minutes. See what you guys can come up with while I'm away. We have resources they don't. Pull in Gideon too."

Murphy stood, then hesitated. "I don't like this,

Abe. It doesn't feel right with Matt not part of the team."

Abe studied Murphy's face. "I know. All we can do is pray for their protection and quick return."

Caleb took the paper Abe handed him. "You're sure about this name?"

Abe hesitated, then said, "About as sure as I can be of anything right now. Any word?"

"Frankie found an older farmer who saw a truck pull into the old campground out that way. He said there were three people in it, two men and a woman, but he couldn't give a lot of details. Frankie's headed that way now with the search team."

"I hope they find them. It's not going to be a very warm night and they're not dressed for it."

Matt stood awkwardly and walked to Sarah. He could see she was ready to collapse. The man stopped him, weapon to his chest. Matt stared at him.

"She's ready to collapse. Now untie me, unless you want her to die." He could see the uncertainty in the man's eyes. Up close, he realized how young the man was, not as old as he thought.

The captor looked between Matt and Sarah and finally moved to untie Matt. "No tricks."

Matt shook his head as he rubbed his wrists. "No tricks. I just want to make sure she's okay." He was motioned forward.

Kneeling by Sarah, he touched her face. She looked up at him through pain-filled eyes. "Oh, sweetheart, I'm sorry." He sat with his back to a tree and gathered her close to him. She closed her eyes and her head went to his shoulder. He could feel her start to relax but she was still tense from the pain.

Darkness descended. Clouds scuttled across the sky, obscuring the moon and stars at time. Matt shivered in the damp coolness and gather Sarah as close as he could to try and keep her warm. Movement in front of him made him look up. Their captor stood there, watching him. Matt stared in amazement as the man shrugged out of his jacket and draped it over Sarah. Their eyes met, and Matt saw the uncertainty.

"You could give yourself up. I'll speak up for you." Matt's voice was low.

The man stopped as he was walking away, then continued his pacing. He thought about where he was and what he had planned for his life. This was not it. He turned to stare at the two sitting beneath the pine. How could he get himself out of this?

Frankie climbed into the camper that they used as a command post and took the coffee handed to him with a quiet thank you. They had found the truck, but it had been stolen the week previous. He watched the activity around him, then ducked to glance through the door towards the east. The sky was lightening and he knew they could soon have the search underway. He turned as the head of the search and rescue team stopped beside him.

"About another half hour and we'll get going. There's a major trail going up, and it looks as if that's the one they took."

"Where does it lead?"

"It heads to the top of the ridge, and then splits.

If you keep going straight, it takes you down the other side and into the next county. If you go to the right, it will lead you to the huge cabin that no one wants to live in and no one wants to claim ownership for."

Frankie's eyes narrowed as he thought. "What would be your best guess as to where they're headed?"

The SAR leader shrugged. "Depends on what they want from them. But if Sarah's in difficulty like you say, then who knows which way they would go? I would suspect they've holed up somewhere overnight."

****

He stood in the open this time, watching the activity at the campground. Had they been found? He hoped so. He still needed to get to Sarah and if she was dead, then he was lost.

Chapter 9

Sarah stirred, feeling the cold and the dampness around her. Matt's head was back against the tree and he seemed to be asleep. She raised her head from his shoulder and looked around. Their captor sat not too far from them, watching. She saw the aloneness that he showed and the uncertainty.

"You could stop this right now." She spoke softly. "Let us go, and come with us. Tell them who put you up to this. We'll put in a good word for you."

The man, who was a lot younger than they thought, stared at her. "I've gone too far."

Sarah shook her head. "Not if you give up now. You haven't killed anyone, have you?" When he shook his head, she held out her hand. "Let me have your weapon and your phone."

He looked down at the weapon he had laid on the ground, then at the phone. He had finally turned the phone off. He felt he had been set up and he really didn't like that feeling. He raised his head again to look at Sarah. "You would really do that for me?" he asked.

She nodded. "I would. You're too young to throw any more of your life away. I'll find you a good lawyer, I know a few, and we'll see what we can work out."

He looked down, and when he looked back up,

she could see the resignation in his face. He picked up his weapon, stopped and handed it to her, then handed her his phone. "Thank you. I don't know why you're doing this."

"Because God wants me to." She looked at him as his face blanked and then he shook his head.

"People don't do that for the likes of me."

"I do, Matt does. We are told to forgive and we must follow Christ's example to forgive. You need healing, my friend, and only Christ can bring you that healing."

The young man, youth really, stared at the ground. "You have no idea how much."

Sarah stood awkwardly and when she had her balance, she laid her hand on his arm. "No, I don't know how much, but God does. When we get back to town, let our pastor come see you. Greg can help you and walk you through the steps you need."

He looked up, almost a sheen of tears in his eyes. "He would do that, for a stranger?"

"What stranger?" Matt spoke from behind Sarah, and startled, the youth looked at him. "We could be friends. As Sarah has said, let us help you. Tell us what you know."

He started to shake his head, then turned and pointed at the trail they had walked up the day before. "Tell me. Who was standing there all night?"

Matt and Sarah exchanged a glance, then Matt asked, "Who?"

"There was a man standing there all night, an older man, dressed in a plaid shirt and jeans. He had a baseball cap on. He never moved the whole night, just stood there.”

Matt and Sarah shared another glance. “How close were you to having to kill us last night?” Sarah asked quietly, her eyes searching the youth’s face.

He blanched. “If the call had come through, I might have. But the call never came. He said if he didn’t call, he would come up himself. And he never came.”

Sarah leaned back on Matt, suddenly feeling in the need of his support. Matt wrapped his arms around her and studied the youth.

“That was an angel sent by God, then, to protect us and to protect you.” Matt could feel Sarah nodding in agreement. “So, let’s head back down. We’ll talk to Caleb for you. And by the way, we really would like to know your name.”

“It’s Erik. I didn’t see any one other than you two, yesterday. He was there but I don’t know what he was doing. He just told me to make sure you two were taken away.”

****

He stood and watched the activity in the campground parking lot. They must know where she is and are going to find her. He raised his eyes to look towards the top of the ridge. She must be up there somewhere. How can I get around them to get to her?

****

Frankie came to a halt as the search team members stopped in front of him. He stepped to the side and looked ahead, shocked to see Matt, Sarah and a young man walking towards them. They looked cold, tired and hungry but otherwise in good shape.

Matt stopped by Frankie, and handed him the weapon and phone. "Don't ask. We want to talk to Caleb about Erik."

Frankie took a look at the young man. "Erik. You're on a first name basis with your kidnapper?"

"What kidnapper?" Sarah brushed by him. "I don't know about anyone else but I'm with friends."

Frankie stared after her, then at Matt. Matt shrugged. Erik looked sheepish and scared, not knowing what he was facing.

"It's okay, Frankie. I'll explain but can we first get down off the mountain and get somewhere warm?"

Frankie exchanged glances with the SAR leader, who shrugged. Frankie hung back to speak with him.

"What's that all about?" the leader asked.

"I have no idea. It's really strange."

"I know you needed our help or you wouldn't have asked. I can't say I've ever had this situation before though and I am not quite sure how to write up the paperwork."

"When you figure it out, let me know, will you? I'll have the same problem as you."

Caleb and Abe both stared at Frankie, not sure if they should take him seriously.

"You mean to tell me, you met them coming back down the ridge, with their captor, who they declared is now their friend?"

Frankie held up his hands. "Don't shoot the messenger. I'm just telling you how is it, Caleb."

Caleb stared past him at where Matt and Sarah were seated, food and hot drinks in front of them. He knew Sarah had insisted the youth she called Erik be given somewhere to clean up and given something to eat and drink. He shook his head. He just didn't get it.

Caleb shook his head. "Did you say you have his phone?"

Frankie nodded. "I already dropped it off at the lab."

Abe turned to Caleb. "Are you done with Matt now?"

Caleb nodded. "He's given a statement and it pretty much matches what Sarah has to say. Somehow I don't think it's what really happened, but they're sticking to what they've given."

"In that case, I'm going to take Matt back to Rebel's. Where are you putting Sarah?"

Caleb ran his hand through his hair in frustration. "Now, that is a very good question. I have no idea where I can put her to keep her out of trouble. It follows her all over the place."

Frankie snickered. "It happens to all the young women in this town. Sooner or later, trouble tracks them down and it's usually without them trying too hard."

"I can take her back to Rebel's and try and keep an eye on her." Abe turned to watch the two again. "Wait a minute. Where'd Sarah go?"

Frankie and Abe spun. Sure enough, Matt was sitting by himself, Sarah nowhere in sight. Eddie had stopped by Matt and they could see him looking towards the front of the department. Matt stood and walked that way, Eddie beside him. The three in Caleb's office moved out to watch was what happening, just in time to see Eddie and Matt disappear out the front door.

"Now where are they going?" Abe strode towards the front of the building and yanked open the door. The two men were nowhere in sight. He stepped down onto the sidewalk and looked around, finally seeing them disappear into a building a few doors down from the department.

Caleb stood beside him. "A lawyer. What would you say the chances are that Sarah has gone to find a lawyer for their 'friend'?"

"I would say very good."

Abe was waiting for Matt outside the building. "Come on, Matt. We're heading home."

Matt hesitated, then nodded. "Did you get a chance to speak with Caleb?"

"Oh, yes I did. Quite a story there." Abe eyes Matt as he unlocked his truck. "Do you really think there are two?"

Matt scanned the area out of habit. "I do. Erik isn't smart enough or old enough to have come up with the plan and there's no way he would have been able to take out our guys. And before you ask, I don't think it's related to Sarah. It's me."

Abe backed out of his parking spot and pulled away. "That's the conclusion we have come up with. Murphy came up with some names and Caleb's men are running them down now."

Matt said a name and Abe's fingers stilled from where he had been tapping them on the steering wheel.

"It's funny you mention that name. Murphy came up with it."

Matt stared ahead. "I still can't figure out why. He had such hatred for me. As far as I recall, I don't know him."

"Somehow, I think you do. Maybe not the name he was using then, but you have to know him somehow. Could he be related to the drunk driver?"

Matt thought about that. "It's possible, I guess, but I don't know why he would be coming after me all these years later."

Sarah sank gratefully down onto the couch in her home. Doug had been out and brought her cats back, and they cuddled close to her. She took the cup of coffee Doug handed her gratefully, with a quiet word of thanks.

"What's going on, Sarah?" Doug was puzzled. Sarah was not acting like the Sarah he knew.

"What do you mean, Doug?"

"That bit with that guy today. That's not like you."

She studied her friend and saw the concern in his face. "I just can't explain it, Doug. It's like God was telling me to forgive him, that He wanted to deal with him, not me, not Matt."

"Are you for real?" Doug jumped up and started to pace. "He kidnapped you, held you captive over night, and you are ready to forgive and forget?"

"That's enough, Doug. One more word and you can leave. God clearly told me to forgive." Sarah rose to her feet, eyes blazing with anger. "Don't ever tell me what to do or feel." She turned her back on him. "I think you need to leave. Now!"

Doug hesitated, then move to the door. He turned to watch his friend. seeing the fatigue in her stance, but seeing something else as well, a determination he had not seen in her before. "Call me, Sarah, if you need me." He waited but she did not respond. Heart sinking, he prayed he had not ruined years' worth of friendship.

Sarah heard the door click behind Doug, moved to make sure the locks were on, and then headed for her bedroom. She needed to clean up and then sleep. She wasn't sure if her brain would shut off enough for her to do so, but she hoped it would. God, please let me sleep tonight. Help me to leave it all in Your hands. Help me to forgive.

Chapter 10

Sarah walked through her house the next morning and out into her back yard. She looked around, relishing the freedom she once more felt, but she knew it wouldn't last for long. Someone was after her and someone else was after Matt. She tried to figure out who was after her and could only come up with one name. She hesitated as she looked towards Doug's home. They had not left each other in good terms last night, he had pushed when she was really tired. She walked down the yard of her home, towards her rose garden, savouring the freshness of the early morning, her feet in her flip-flops getting wet from the dew. She stopped as she looked over the roses and drew in the sweet scent of them. The aroma reminded her of her grandmother, who loved wearing rose perfume.

She turned and studied her home, seeing the two cats standing up at the patio door. She didn't feel safe there any more in her childhood home and she always had done so. What made the difference now? She started as she heard a voice and turned. Doug stood at the fence, watching her, an uncertain look on his face.

"Are you okay, Sarah?" he asked.

She nodded as she walked towards him. "I am. I'm sorry about last night, Doug. I was just so tired."

"It's okay. I shouldn't have questioned you. I just wanted to make sure you were okay."

"I am, for now."

"What do you mean, for now?"

"Have you ever felt a sense of impending doom, knowing something was going to happen, you had no idea what, and that you had no way of stopping it? That's how I feel right now." She glanced up at him. "I need to go talk to Caleb and Eddie. I have a name to give them, and I am not sure if it's the right thing to do or not."

"Have you prayed about it?" Doug asked. When she nodded, he continued, "Then if you have prayed about it and God has given you peace, then you know it's the right thing to do."

She nodded. "It's just that it affects more than me, this person. I've held onto the name for years. I guess it's time for me to let it go."

Doug watched as she walked away, her limp not as pronounced this morning. He prayed for his friend, that she would have peace about the step she was taking. His heart feared for her, though. She was right, he could feel the impending doom. He turned and headed for his home as his pager went off. Work was calling, and he prayed that it would be an easy call.

Abe watched as his team gathered in the conference room, studying Matt in particular. He seemed distracted, and Abe needed him to have his full attention on what they were doing.

Discussion and instructions and planning for the upcoming security assignment in a neighbouring city finished, Abe asked Murphy and Matt to stay behind.

Matt was restless, pacing the area, not like himself at all.

"Matt, are you with us 100%?" Abe was concerned.

Matt looked up, realizing what Abe was asking, and nodded. "I have to be, Abe. You are all depending on me. God will help me to put aside what's happened."

Murphy watched him. "What actually happened up there, Matt? No one has really explained it."

Matt stared at his two friends. "I'm not sure if I can even explain it." He went on to describe what had happened. "The strangest thing was the man Erik saw standing at the trail head, keeping anyone away."

"A man?" Abe and Murphy exchanged glances. "I thought it was only the three of you there."

Matt nodded. "Just three you could see. Erik was adamant there was another person there. Sarah and I think it was an angel."

Murphy and Abe shared a glance.

"An angel?" Abe watched for Matt's response as he questioned him.

"An angel. He was positive there was another man there, standing in the path. So, you tell me, what would you think?" He turned to his friends. "Is it possible?"

"It's entirely possible, Matt." Murphy was choosing his words carefully. "We know God has angels around us, and He may chosen to reveal one to this young man.”

Matt shook his head. “I still don’t get it.” He walked out of the room, leaving the two behind staring after him.

“Are you sure about this, Sarah?” Caleb watched Sarah’s face as she stood in front of him in the conference room.

“I am. It’s time. I just need to empty the safety deposit box and then I will bring it to you.” She turned to leave, but stopped when he called her name.

“Sarah, let one of us go with you. If this person has any suspicions about what you are planning, you can be sure he will take steps.”

She nodded. “I know. I have felt his eyes watching me more and more and the sense of evil has been growing.”

Frankie followed Sarah into the bank and waited while she asked for her box. He watched as she hesitated to open it.

She looked up at him from studying the box. “I feel like I am opening up something that I can never close again.”

“You are, but you need to do this.”

She pulled out the documents and flash drive from the box, stuffed them into an envelope and handed it to Frankie. “Here, you take it. Just don’t let anyone see you have it.”

Frankie watched her face and saw the fear there. “I won’t.” He folded the envelope lengthwise and putting it into an inside pocket on his jacket, waited while she returned the box, and then followed her out of the bank.

****

He watched from inside the bank. He had just happened to be there that morning and saw her enter. What had she pulled from back there? Forgetting why he was there, he followed her to the department and watched as she entered, followed by Frankie.

Chapter 11

Abe finished his paperwork and tucked it away in his briefcase, setting his briefcase down by his seat. He looked around at the five men with him in the plane. Ian and Murphy being in the cockpit. They had done well, the assignment was over, and they were headed home. He rested his head back and closed his eyes. This was the last overseas assignment he would take. The timing was right to stop.

His eyes opened and rested on Matt. What had actually happened on the ridge that night? Was it really an angel? He didn't doubt it was possible but who had the angel then kept away from them?

Murphy dropped down into the seat beside him, watching Matt as well.

"Who do you think is really responsible for what is going on?" Murphy's voice was puzzled. It hurt the whole team when one was in danger.

Abe shrugged. "I have no idea. I'm hoping Caleb or Eddie come up with something on that name. Other than that, I really don't know who to look at."

Matt was deep in thought, trying to determine who would be after him. His mind went back over all their assignments, and then drifted back over the years. He could vaguely remember someone threatening him years ago, but couldn't drag up the name. He had never told anyone about it, but as he tried to work it through, it became clear. He knew who it was and how it connected to him. But how had he tracked him down? He had left his home town and only had contact with his mother, even that limited.

He turned to find Abe watching him. "I know who it is. It has nothing to do with the team or any assignments we have been on."

"Why do you say that?" Abe wasn't ready to let go of the name Murphy had come up with.

"Because he threatened me, and anyone I was close to, years ago. That's why I never go see my mother." He wrote a name down on the back of a business card he pulled from his pocket. "Pass this on to Caleb. I think you'll find he's in the area."

Abe took the card and as he turned it over to read the name, a chill came over him, a sense of foreboding and evil stronger than he had ever felt before. The name struck deep within him. He knew that man, knew the evil he was capable of. His eyes raised to Matt's and saw the devastation there.

"I know this man, Matt. He has tried to take over Rebel's on numerous occasions. He has set up a rival security firm and has been responsible for many lives lost." Abe stopped speaking, lost in thought. "I never realized that you knew him."

Matt shook his head. "I thought I had left him behind when I moved across the country. I guess I haven't. But I still don't get why he's after me. I don't remember anything in my past dealings with him to explain that."

Abe tucked the card into his shirt pocket. "I'll take to Caleb when we get back."

Caleb studied the file that Sarah had handed Frankie. "Does Sarah realize how strong a case she has here?"

Frankie shook his head. "I don't think she does nor do I think she really cares. She just wants it over with. Her father had been collecting evidence for years, and I suspect that's why the man went after Sarah, to make her dad stop. But that time, though, her parents had already moved away."

"Is she still here?"

Frankie shook his head. "No, she left as soon as she knew I was heading to your office."

Caleb stood and headed for the conference room. They had more room there to lay out the material. As they sorted it through it, they began to understand why Sarah had never given it to them. The scope of the material was immense.

Eddie stopped as he saw them. He picked up one of the documents, then stilled. "Do you know what you have here?"

Frankie shook his head. "We've just started sorting it out."

Eddie stared at the paper, then reached over to the other table for the list Abe had given them. "We have the connection. The name Abe gave you and this man—they're brothers. Rumour has it that their father was connected to gangs but no one could ever prove it.

"Where's Sarah?" he looked around as he asked that.

"She left after giving me this material."

They looked up as a knock came at the door. Abe stood there, the business card Matt had handed him in his hand. "Is this a bad time?" he asked.

"No." Caleb shook his head. "What do you have there?" As he took the card and read the name, his heart sank. They were right. The two cases were connected.

"They're related, aren't they? I can tell by the look on your face. Matt remembered who it was today. He's been blocking it."

"How does Matt know him?" Eddie was curious to see how the two cases connected.

Abe told them. The shock of the three men's faces told of the devastation they knew Matt had to feel.

"I'll make sure Matt stays with one of my guys all the time. What about Sarah?"

"Now that we know the connection, you can be sure we'll do everything we can to keep Sarah safe. But she's going to fight us on this." Caleb thought through how they would manage to keep her safe. "It's going to be difficult."

Frankie dropped the papers he was holding and headed for the door. "I'll see if I can talk her into some protection. Don't hold your breath."

Caleb turned to study the conference room, knowing that once again it would be used as a staging area for the investigation. This time, though, it seemed as if the need was greater and more urgent and the ramifications deeper. Lord, how do we do this? How do we keep everyone safe until we can find these two men? It's going to be tough and only You are the one who can direct where we go.

Caleb turned as Eddie spoke. "I wish Ben were here. He always had the insight into these investigations that we don't."

Caleb nodded. "He has agreed to work as a consultant. If only he and Marg were home, I would call him in."

Sarah stood back as Frankie entered her home. She could already tell she wasn't going to like what he had to say.

"I just made some fresh coffee, if you want some." Her eyebrows raised questioningly, then she turned to lead the way to the kitchen. She swept her paperwork into a ticy pile, leaving to set it in her office.

Frankie had poured their coffee and was standing looking out her patio door when she returned. She picked up hers and then nodded at the door.

"Let's go outside, Frankie. I don't want to stay in."

Frankie followed her down the steps and towards her rose garden.

"So, why are you here?"

Frankie took a sip of his coffee and realized as he swallowed it that it was still a little too hot to do that. "Caleb sent me. We've identified the men after both you and Matt."

Sarah nodded, then turned. "Two men. That's what you thought all along."

Frankie agreed. "But there's more to it. They're related to one another."

Sarah stopped walking and stared at him, then her gaze went into the distance. "Related? So how do two men, related to one another, become our culprits or villains or instigators, or whatever some novelist would call them?" She sounded outraged.

Frankie gave a short bark of laughter. "Love your sense of humour, Sarah. As to the connection, we're working on that." When he gave the names and the connection to Matt, she stared at him, horrified at the thought of how Matt must be feeling.

"So, I've been right all along, and so has Dad."

"You two have been. That material you gave us will go a long way to prosecuting him." Frankie turned in a circle, feeling the evil near him. "We need to get you somewhere safe, Sarah. I don't think your house will do it."

Sarah turned to her house. "No, it won't. I have had the feeling for months now of being watched. And it's almost as if someone has been in my house, just subtle things. Nothing definite that I can point a finger to."

Frankie slanted her a glance. "Why don't I have one of our crime team guys come over, just as a friend, and go through your home? We can always use the pretext that they're coming to visit Doug. They're all friends."

"I don't like pretending, Frankie. And I would rather not involve Doug if I can help it. He already hovers too much."

Frankie agreed with her but didn't add his thought that she needed someone to hover and that someone seemed to becoming more and more Matt. They made a cute couple, he thought. Lord, if they're the ones meant for each other, protect them.

"I still have to work, Frankie." She turned to him. "We have way too much for me to be off."

He nodded. "We'll work it out."

Chapter 12

Matt watched as Abe stood talking with Caleb near the gate to Rebel's. He was frustrated beyond words. Here, he thought he was safe, was away from that man but he had tracked him down. He thought of his mother and prayed she was safe.

Joseph spoke from beside him. "Now what, Matt? Has Abe said?"

Matt shook his head. "No, and I have a feeling I'm already not going to like it."

Joseph laughed. "No, I don't think you will. It's not fun being on the other side of the coin. At least here you're in your home."

"I am, but what about Sarah? She's had to leave the only home she's ever known, just because of that guy."

"She'll manage. She's a lot stronger that she looks."

Sarah walked past them towards the two men at the gate. She was not happy. Abe looked up, saw her and said something to Caleb. Matt and Joseph watched the discussion, seeing the frustration in the three.

"Who do you think is going to win this one?" Joseph was amused. He was thinking it would be

Sarah.

"Judging by the look on Caleb's face, it will be him, but I wouldn't rule out Sarah." Murphy had come to stand beside them. "She's a spitfire, that she is. Are you sure you're going to be able to handle her, Matt?"

Matt ignored them, a sudden sense of evil and pending doom sending chills down his back. He spun to study the rocky area around the compound. He didn't like it. Someone was there watching but which one of them was he watching?

Murphy watched as Sarah came towards them and then stopped, looking at them.

"I'm headed into work and I'm told someone has to come with me. I would rather no one did, but I don't have much of a choice. So who is it?"

The three men looked at one another, not speaking. Sarah stared at them, then walked away. Joseph ran after her.

"I'll go, Sarah. Just give us a minute to get the vehicle ready."

She spun, shaking her head. "My car. It's got my gear. And if you're not at it in three minutes, I'm gone."

Joseph stared at her, then shook his head. Really, three minutes? He headed for her car and stood waiting for her.

She looked over his clothes. "You're going to be filthy by day's end, you know."

He shrugged. "Won't be the first time or the last."

Joseph leaned on the broom he had been using that afternoon to sweep up the job site for John and Sarah. He had enjoyed the change, getting away from what he normally did. His admiration for the two cousins had grown. They worked well together, seeming to know what the other wanted or was doing before they spoke.

Sarah came towards, fatigue in her steps. "Thanks, Joseph. That means a lot, you sweeping up for us. It's usually John or I at the end of the day."

"No problem. Are you about done here now?"

She nodded. "We are. John loading up his equipment and tools and then we're done. Another project completed."

"So where will you be tomorrow then?"

Sarah thought about the jobs they had on the go and then shrugged. "Wherever I'm needed, I guess. I usually go out and do quotes but John has taken that on for now."

Sarah tugged out her phone and looked at the number.

"What's up, Doug?"

"Not much. Just wondering how you are?"

"I'm okay. Just frustrated at not being home. Can you look after Spider and Miss Muffet until I can get them?"

He gave a longsuffering sigh. "I suppose. And I also suppose Spider will want to ride around on my shoulders?"

Sarah laughed at the picture his words brought to mind. "Of course she will. If you need supplies, I get them from Ashling's folks' store."

"Okay. As long as you're okay?"

"About as well as I can be right now. Thanks, Doug."

Joseph, listening to the conversation, wondered at how deep the affection went between them.

Sarah, turning, caught the look on his face. "Don't worry, Joseph, I won't hurt Matt. Doug and I have been best friends since we were two, growing up in homes side by side, with parents who are good friends with one another. I don't think I'll ever forgive for taking home my favourite sand shovel though."

Joseph stared at her. "How did you know what I was thinking?"

She shrugged. "Someone else asked that a while ago. I have no idea." She walked towards John and after a brief conversation, headed back to her car. Joseph reached for her keys, and after a minute, she handed them to him.

"Just don't forget to put the seat back to where I have it. I'll never reach the pedals if you don't."

Joseph laughed as he drove away, eyes scanning the area. He could feel the evil following him, getting closer as he drove toward Rebel's. He sensed Sarah's agitation as well.

"Sarah, I think we're being followed, but I can't see which car."

"I know we're being followed. He just won't let up, even though I don't have the material any more."

"What material?"

"Dad and I had been amassing evidence on a man in town and I finally turned it over to Caleb. He's working on it now."

Joseph's eyes traveled to the side mirror as he saw a truck coming up in the passing lane. He didn't like how fast the truck was coming or the feeling he had. He scanned the area to his right and it was clear. There was an exit just up ahead and he spun the wheel, cutting across the lane of traffic to take it. The oncoming cars were back far enough that he could make the exit but the truck that was overtaking him had to keep going.

"Do you know that truck, Sarah?"

She shook her head. "Fancy driving there. Can you teach me?"

Joseph stared at her in disbelief, then returned his eyes to the road, shaking his head. "That's all you can say, teach me?"

Sarah laughed. "It wasn't our time, Joseph. God has control of this. I just have to keep reminding myself of that."

"You're right. We have to keep reminding ourselves of that when we're out on assignment."

He watched as the police officers approached his door. He had been expecting them for years. Sarah must have turned over whatever she and her father had had.

"Edwin Benson, you're under arrest." Eddie began to list the charges.

Edwin Benson withered in front of them. At one

time, he had been a powerful man in town, but no longer. He stared ahead as he was handcuffed and led from his building, passerbys stopping to stare and comment, no longer afraid of his power. Head high, he knew he would be out shortly and then he would go after her.

Chapter 13

Caleb nodded as Eddie entered his office. "He's been arrested?"

"He has, but he thinks he'll be out right away. He likely will too, even with the attempted murder charge. Our people are searching his premises now. They're finding lots of evidence. He didn't get rid of a thing."

Caleb shook his head. "He has always had that arrogance about him, that he was untouchable. Can we tie him to the officer's death?"

Eddie nodded. "We can. That should go a long ways to keeping him in jail for now. I spoke with the judge and he will be setting a very high bail, given the evidence and charges." He watched Caleb. "So, who tells Sarah? You know she's going to want to go home right away."

"I know she will but she's still a target. It's known around town that Matt is interested in her, even though they haven't been seen together much."

"Word does get around, doesn't it? I guess that means she stays where she is."

Caleb stared at the wall on the other side of the room from his desk. "She will have to. And she won't like it. I can see her running."

"Wouldn't be the first one. Will Matt go with

her?"

Caleb shrugged. "It depends on if she tells him she's going or not. Abe will try and keep them both close to Rebel's but I know Sarah well enough to know she'll be out working, unless we can get John to send her away on a vacation, and I can't see that happening any time soon." He brought his eyes back to Eddie. "Where do we stand on the investigation with Matt?"

"Now there's an investigation. Every time we track down evidence and confirm it, more evidence crops up. This guy, he's good but not as good as us. Our IT people are digging deep into it and tracking through the companies he's set up. It's a lot bigger than what we thought. He's after Matt for more than just being who he is, he's after him for revenge. We're trying to get a handle on that."

Sarah turned her head as Abe came towards her. Rebecca had invited her over for supper and the two women had been sitting in the back yard, just talking. Rebecca had had to go take a phone call, and Abe took advantage of his sister being otherwise occupied. He sat on the swing beside Sarah and didn't say a word. He wasn't quite sure how to begin.

"He's been arrested?" Sarah's voice was quiet and sad.

"He has, Sarah. There's a lot of evidence being gathered from his home and business locations." Abe paused, turning to look at her. "He hasn't talked yet, but we do know now why he ran you down."

"He did it himself?" Sarah was shocked, having thought all along that he had paid someone to do it.

"He did. He wanted to hurt your father for standing up to him over building code issues for years. He was greedy and he saw hurting you as a way to get back at your Dad. Plain and simple, that's how it was. He also saw you and John following in the integrity your Dad showed and he wanted to hurt both of you. If he hadn't been able to get to you, he would have gone after John."

"Man's depravity at work again. I know God has a plan for this and has had all along. I am thankful it happened though."

Abe studied her. "What do you mean?"

"It took Tom out of my life, and before you ask, yes I know Doug flattened him for me."

Abe looked up as he saw Ian step out onto the deck. "I have to go take care of something, Sarah, but know this. We want you to stay with us until this is all over. Matt is still a target and I know you are becoming important to him. You will be used to get to him. To keep you safe, we need to keep you close to us. Caleb has asked us to step in with security. I have put off some security assignments for now, my friends are willing and happy to step in for me; I would do the same for them. Our talk is not yet finished."

She started to refuse, then caught the glint in Abe's eye. He expected her to refuse his protection and was amused that she would even debate it.

"Then, thank you, Abe, I will be glad to stay. John will want me to go in for part days. Joseph did amazing grunt work today for us." She laughed as the expression on his face.

"You're as bad as Rebecca, you know that, Sarah? Welcome to our family."

Abe stood and walked back to the house, leaving Sarah pondering what he meant by that last comment. The family? As far as she knew she was just a guest.

Rebecca rejoined her, studying her. "Did Abe ask you to stay with us?"

Sarah laughed. "He did and he was taken aback when I agreed."

Rebecca joined in her laughter. "Good for you. He needs to be taken down a peg or two every once in a while." She turned her head to study Sarah. "You do know that Matt is falling in love with you, don't you?"

Sarah gave a small smile. "That's what everyone is telling me. I haven't heard it from him yet."

Rebecca shook her head. "You may not for a while. He's had a lot in his past he has had to deal with and he needs to find forgiveness for those who hurt him before he can heal and move on. You are helping with that, Sarah. I see it more and more every day. What you went through has taught you a lot."

"Like it did you, too, Rebecca." Sarah leaned her head back and studied the night sky. "Do you ever question why Go let us go through what we did?"

Rebecca shook her head. "Not really. It

wouldn't have done any good, any way."

Matt waited the next afternoon for Joseph and Sarah to return. Sarah had had to be on a site for an inspection that afternoon as well as some other issues to deal with, and Joseph had elected himself to go with her. She teased him that he only wanted to do grunt work again, and he just grinned.

Ian walked by as Matt paced near the garage. "They're not back yet?"

Matt shook his head. "They should have been back 45 minutes ago, and I can't reach either on their cells."

"I don't like that. Did Joseph say where they were heading?"

Matt shook his head. "He wasn't sure. Sarah had a few places to stop at today, minor repairs and some quotes."

"Come on, let's go tell Abe we're off and then we'll see if we can find them."

Chapter 14

Eddie eased out of his car at the construction site. There were no workers around now, it was getting late. He walked towards the partially constructed home and saw Joseph's car.

Reaching for his phone, he called Abe. "I have Joseph's car at the last site addressJohn gave us. I'm calling for back up before I go any further. Keep Matt away for now until we see what's up."

"Easier said than done, Eddie. I don't think we're going to be able to."

"I'll be setting up a perimeter more than likely. I'll call in a few."

Drawing his weapon, Eddie walked cautiously towards the home and around the outside. Seeing nothing, he stepped inside, his flashlight shining through the rooms. Nothing. No Joseph. No Sarah. He walked down the rough construction steps to the basement and searched. Nothing again. The same for the second floor.

He stepped outside, frustrated, as the first of his back up arrived. The officers spread out to continue their search. A call and Eddie ran for the back of the property.

Ian pulled to the side of the street as an ambulance raced by him, lights and sirens activated. He pulled back into the line of traffic and then turned, following the ambulance. Out of the corner of his eye, he could see the tenseness in Matt.

"Stay here, Matt." Ian's hand rested on Matt's arm. "Let me find out what's going on."

Matt shrugged off the hand. "Not a chance, Ian." He pushed open his door and then strode towards the activity.

Abe stopped him before he got too far. "Sarah's not here, Matt. We've found Joseph. Someone got the drop on him and left him bound and gagged behind the construction material. He's mad, but relatively unscathed. He can't tell us what happened to Sarah. They were together when he was hit from behind."

Hours later, Matt stood, leaning against Eddie's car, hands deep into his jeans pockets, watching the activity. Where was Sarah? Lord, please protect her. Keep her safe. If it's me they want, I'll trade.

Doug handed him a jacket and he shrugged into it with a quiet word of thanks.

"No word yet, Doug?"

Doug shook his head. "Nothing had come in when I left. How's Joseph?"

"They took him to have him checked out at Emerge but he was not a happy man for sure. Whoever it is must have been following them and waited until they were on their own. Joseph said everyone else was gone and Sarah had just stepped back to check one more measurement."

Doug's eyes roamed the area, catching the movements of the investigators. "They won't find a lot here. There are too many tracks." He turned to look behind him. "It's a pretty isolated area, too. Not a lot of traffic in the evening."

"I know. That's why he picked this." Matt stared at the ground, not sure how to continued. "I'm sorry, Doug. We were doing our best."

Doug turned to study him, head tilted to the side so he could see Matt's face better. "Your team has done the best they could. Nothing has been straightforward or sane about this guy. Frankie said they're narrowing down areas where he might be, but even that fluctuates from day to day."

He watched as his man carried Sarah to the room he had prepared for her on the second floor. There was no way she could get out, he thought. Windows were sealed and there was a double-keyed deadbolt on the door. He stepped over to the bed to study her, taking in the dark circles under her eyes and the paleness of her skin. She had fought them, the evidence of that fight in the bruises on her face and on her wrists. He reached out a finger to touch the dried blood at the corner of her mouth and she flinched at his touch She would serve her purpose and then be disposed of, just like Matt.

He turned and left the room, waiting until it had been locked before he spoke. "Bring her food and water in about an hour. We will wait until tomorrow to make start our campaign."

The man nodded and then trod down the back steps to the kitchen. His employer would be expecting his dinner soon and brooked no delays in it being served to him.

Abe watched as Matt sank heavily into the chair in the conference room at the police department. He turned from him, unable for the moment to face the devastation on his friend's face. Frankie was watching Matt too and when Abe turned, motioned him to follow him out of the room.

"He's really hurting, Abe."

"I know. I just wish we could make it better, but it won't happen overnight. Any word on where the man is?"

Frankie shook his head. "We're still trying to confirm residence locations. He has them hidden deep in numbered companies."

"Has Gideon been helping?"

Frankie nodded. "Even he's run into a few roadblocks. This guy is good." He pointed at the conference room with his chin. "Take him home. There won't be anything coming through tonight. It's usually a day or two before anything like a ransom demand is made."

"I doubt it will be a ransom demand."

"Not in the sense you mean. It will be a ransom demand in the sense that we have to give them something to get Sarah back, or I should say someone."

"Matt."

Frankie nodded. "And we have to prevent that in some way." He stepped back so he could see through the door. Matt was slumped in his chair, head down. "Take him home, Abe. We'll call if we need either one of you."

Matt paced his living room, worry for Sarah uppermost in his mind. He stopped as Ian stepped into his path and handed him a cup of coffee.

"You'll wear a path there, Matt."

"I know. I just wish I knew where she was. If he has her....." Matt's voice dropped away.

"Sit." Ian waited until Matt did with a glare directed his way. "God knows where she is and has her in His care. Talk to me, Matt. You're hurting in more ways than one. Tell me about your family and this man you suspect." Ian's eyes caught Abe and Murphy stepping through the door, and then sitting quietly down in the living room out of Matt's sight.

Matt's eyes slid closed. "I don't know if I can tell you about it. It hurts so much. If I do tell it to you, I won't ever repeat it."

Ian nodded. "I understand. Talk to me, Matt."

The three men in the room with him listened as for the first time ever Matt poured out his heart about what his life had been like. Their hearts broke for the boy who had lost so much and for the man who had suffered so as a child. The other four members of his team of friends sat out of sight in the kitchen. They had all gathered to support him, knowing it would be a difficult night for him to get through.

Matt's friends gathered around him when he was finished, prayers raised to heaven for him. When he stood, he staggered, emotionally and physically spent. Ian caught him as he fell and helped him to his bedroom, shutting the door behind him as Matt sank down onto his bed.

Abe turned as Ian came back to the living room,

shaking his head at what Matt had revealed. "I'll go talk to Caleb in the morning. Make sure one of you stay close to Matt. This was bad enough but now with Sarah gone, it's going to be even worse."

Chapter 15

Sarah stirred, careful not to move her head too much. It was pounding in pain, and when she opened her eyes, she could only squint. She tried to focus on what was around her but lost the battle and slipped once more into oblivion. She didn't hear the door unlock or the quiet footsteps that approached where she lay, nor hands setting down a tray with food and water and taking away the tray from the previous night. The man studied her, regret in his eyes for the beating his employer's driver had inflicted on her. His own eyes were opening to what was going on around him, and he no longer liked who he was. He wanted out but he knew he would pay with his life if he tried.

He looked up at the window and then back down at Sarah. Somehow, he would get her away from the monster downstairs and protect her. He turned and walked away, locking the door behind him, treading down the back steps to the kitchen. His mind was working, trying to find a way but at the moment he didn't see a way.

The man worked away in his home office, shredding and sorting. Somehow he knew his time here was short and he didn't want a trail of evidence left behind. He looked up as his man came to the door.

"She's still out, sir."

"She wasn't hit that hard, was she?" The accusation stung.

"No, sir, I don't think so. I don't know why she's still out."

"Go. Check on her. I will want to see her in about an hour. If she's not awake, wake her."

Abruptly dismissed, the man turned and drawing a deep breath once again made his way to Sarah's room. This time, she was awake and sitting on the side of the bed. Her eyes mere slits as she looked at him, she tried to take in as much as she could.

"Here, take these." She was handed painkillers but instead of taking them, she dropped them on the tray. "Take them."

She shook her head and regretted it. "I can only take certain medications and unless I know what it is I don't take any. Where am I, anyway?"

"He wants to see you in about 45 minutes. The bathroom is through there. There are also clean clothes for you to put on."

Sarah glared at his back as he exited. Put on clean clothes? She didn't think so. She stood, carefully waiting until she had her balance and then stepped to the door and tried it. It was locked. She stopped at the bathroom door and turning on the water to as hot as she could handle, she washed as best she could. She picked up the clothes and looked at them, then threw them down. Absolutely not was she putting them on. They were not her style and she would only be seen dead in them, and she highly doubted that she was to be killed just yet.

The man was back and, other than a raised eyebrow when he looked at Sarah, led her down to the study. The elderly man looked up as she came in and then ignored her. She stood for a few minutes watching him, and then wandered around the room. She could feel his eyes on her but she refused to look at him.

"Sit."

"Excuse me?" She spun and stared at him.

"I said, sit."

Sarah stood, refusing to move towards the chair he was pointing at. He glared at her and once more ordered her to sit. When she refused again, his hand raised, and she felt her arm grasped in a tight fashion and she was dragged forward and shoved into the chair. Through the hair that had fallen across her face, she raised her eyes to see the man from the night before. Not this time, she thought, no, not this time. I won't let him beat me again.

She turned to the man sitting at the desk. "So, what do you want from me?" She had decided earlier she would take the offensive. She wasn't going to sit back and let him bully her.

"Feisty, are you? We'll see how long that lasts." The man leaned back in his chair and watched to see what emotions would come to her face. He used people's emotions to best them, to get what he wanted. Sarah's face remained blank, her eyes watchful. His eyes narrowed. Finally, he thought, a worthy opponent, and a woman at that.

"So, are you going to tell me? Because if you're not, I'm out of here."

"Not likely, little lady. I have a plan for you and it doesn't include you leaving just yet. You are going to send a message to the police here."

She shook her head. "Sorry, that's not happening."

She felt fingers digging into her arm and she was yanked from the chair. Please, Lord, she cried, give me the strength I need to get through this. I can't do this. She felt the release of her anxiety and relaxed. No matter what happened, God was with her.

Twenty minutes later, Sarah sat once more in the chair, her face more battered and bruised. She could feel the pain from the right side of her chest as she breathed and hoped no ribs had been broken.

The man stared at her. She hadn't given in, not one inch. He had finally stopped his driver. Beatings weren't going to make her do what he wanted.

The driver set up the video camera in front on her, and she carefully raised her head to watch. She had an idea of what was coming, but the pain was drawing her into it. She had been there before when she had been run down. She had to give in to it, to get relief.

She was handed a paper to hold and her hands were adjusted to the right height. She knew what they were doing. They were sending a message, she hoped to Caleb and not Matt, and somehow she had to let them know she was okay and where she was, if her brain would work enough to let her do that. She wiggled the fingers on her right hand carefully.

Good, she thought, they hadn't seen her. If only the camera rolled for long enough for her to get her message through, Doug would know what she was saying.

"Caleb!"

Caleb looked up as Eddie rushed into the conference room towards him.

"I just got a message about Sarah."

"Sarah? Is she okay?"

Eddie shook his head. "I don't know. All the message said was that a video would be coming and we needed to follow the instructions exactly if we wanted to see her again."

Their eyes meeting, both men's hearts sank.

"Is she still alive, though?" Caleb breathed the thought for both of them.

Eddie's phone dinged, indicated a text message. "I can only pray she is."

He pulled up the message and saw it was a video. Opening the video, with Caleb standing shoulder to shoulder with him, they watched as Sarah stared at the camera, battered and bruised, but with a calmness about her. They read the sign as they watched, knowing it would not be good.

"Wait a minute, what's she doing?" Caleb had Eddie stop the video. "She's looking down at her right hand, very quickly, but just long enough to catch our attention. She's up to something."

Eddie looked at her right hand as he started the video again. "She's moving it. She's trying to signal us." He thought, then said, "We need Doug. Those two had a language of their own when they were kids. It involved their fingers— spelling or words or something like that.”

Chapter 16

Doug leaned back against the wall, arms crossed, as he stared intently at the large computer screen. Eddie had uploaded the video to the computer, and Doug knew computer techs were already working on it, trying to trace it. His eyes narrowed, he worked to understand what she was saying with her hand. She was moving carefully, he knew, so she wouldn't be seen. He heard the noise and movement around him but blocked it out.

Frankie met Matt and Ian outside the closed door. He didn't want Matt seeing what Sarah looked like but he didn't know if he could stop him from going in. Of course, he could pull rank and say it was a police investigation and Matt was too deeply involved, but he knew that Abe and his team were working as hard as they were to try and find Sarah.

"Matt, before you go in, I need to talk to you."

Matt's eyes were locked on the door, and then he looked over at Frankie, anguish evident in his very posture. "Is she alive? That's all I want to know."

Frankie took a deep breath, then nodded. "So far, at the time of the video, she's alive. She's battered but she's alive. She's managed to send a message to Doug, and he's in there now trying to determine what she's saying."

Matt's shoulders slumped in relief as h

scrubbed hands down his face, eyes feeling gritty from lack of sleep. "Can I see the video, Frankie?"

Frankie shared a look with Ian, then turned. "I need to run that by Caleb, Matt. If he says no, then I can't let you. It's part of our investigation. Ian, you'll find coffee in the break room. I'll find you there."

Sarah slowly opened her eyes. She was back in the room she had been assigned. She ached all over, and the headache was barely tolerable. She sensed movement, and turned her eyes to look. He stood watching her, then he stooped to feel her head, replacing the warm cloth with a cold one.

"Sarah, I was to your home. He doesn't know. I brought you some clean clothes and here is your medications." His voice was low. "I am going to try and find a way to get you out of here."

He helped Sarah to sit up, waiting as she steadied herself, and then drew pillows behind her to brace her. He handed her a glass of water and then, at her nod, shook some of the tablets into her hand.

"What's your name?" Sarah's voice was soft and rough.

"It's Spence, Sarah." He watched as she leaned back and closed her eyes. "It may be a day or two until I can get you away. I have the only key to the door, so you won't be disturbed. I'll be back in about an hour with some food for you."

She waited, knowing it would take about thirty minutes this time for the medication to work, if it even did. She reached for the clothes he had left. How had he got into her house? She would need to ask him.

An hour later, showered and in clean clothes, Sarah stood at the window, keeping her balance with her hand braced on the window frame. She was on the second floor and there was no way she could make it down to the ground, even if she could get the window open, and that she couldn't do. She could feel the panic and fear rising in her once again. How long would they keep her alive until Matt showed up and show up she knew he would.

Her thoughts turned to the man in the study, and her eyes narrowed as she turned to gaze around the room. If she was right, her problems and Matt's were related after all. She sighed, knowing there wasn't anything she could do about it right now.

Frankie came to find Ian and Matt. At Matt's look, he shook his head. "Sorry, Matt. Caleb said no."

Matt nodded. "I figured he would. I don't want to interfere in the investigation and have this monster get away because I did." He looked up at Frankie as Frankie seated himself across the table from him. The room was empty for once, and Matt suspected Frankie had something to do with that. He had to swallow hard to get past the lump in his throat before he could speak. "So where do we go from here?"

"Caleb's in the planning stages right now. Our computer techs have been able to narrow down an area where we think she is, but it's not definite yet. The video has specifically asked that you meet with this man and if you do, then Sarah will be released."

Matt looked up and went to speak, but Frankie's

hand was up in the air to stop him. "No, we're not doing that yet. We'll get another message from him, likely today, with more information as to where and when. Until we do, we're locking you up somewhere they can't find you. They can find you at your home, they could find you at Sarah's or Doug's. Abe and Gideon are working on a place now."

Ian watched as Frankie stood and walked away. "Let them plan where to put you, Matt. You know how it works. It's just going to be hard on you being on the other side of the coin this time."

Matt was frustrated and it showed as he got up and paced. "I know. I don't like this. If it is him, do I really want to meet him? I always felt there was someone else involved."

"Why do you say that?" Ian tilted his head to watch Matt's reaction to the question.

Matt shrugged, not even sure himself. "It's just a feeling I've had all along. Sometimes he would be okay and then he would get a phone call or meet someone or go on a trip, and the abuse would start. He didn't like it when I got old enough to stand up to him for Mom and I." Matt thought for a minute. "There was never any physical abuse, just emotional, psychological, whatever fancy name they have for it now."

Eddie had his phone in his hand as he tracked down Caleb, Doug by his side. Doug's second-in-command of the ETF had taken over for the day so Doug could be freed up to work with Eddie. "Got another one, Caleb."

They watched the video Eddie had had

uploaded to the computer, Doug with a puzzled look on his face.

"There's something wrong about this. This wasn't filmed today."

Caleb looked at him, then his head swivelled to study the video. "What do you mean?"

"It's just not right. I know she has the same clothes on but the seating, her posture, everything is the same as the one from yesterday."

Eddie took a closer look. "He's right, Caleb. They must have done the two videos back to back. Is she saying anything this time, Doug?"

Doug watched her hands. "No, she's not. I don't think they caught on but I don't think she has the ability to communicate that way in this video, based on the beating it looks like she took." He winced as he studied his friend's face and wished he could take her place. God, please protect her. Help us to get to her and save her.

"That's what I thought, too." Eddie looked around the room and then beckoned one of the women over. "Take a look at this video, Sue. Tell us your impressions."

Sue Walters was one of the best on their team of investigators for finding the nuances of body language.

"Let me see the first video first, then this one. After that, I want them run side by side at slow motion."

She studied the videos, making notes as she watched. The men stood back, letting her work, knowing she would give them her honest opinion. Caleb looked up as Abe stepped into the room, raising a hand to acknowledge hm.

Sue finally sat back, deep in thought. She turned to the men waiting. "I don't like this, Caleb. They did both of them yesterday, it looks like one right after the other. In the second one, she's barely holding on to the sign. That means she's barely holding on at all. She's been through a lot and I would guess she was beaten when they took her and then severely beaten again before the first video, judging by the by the colouring of the bruising and the fresh lacerations. Doug, she's your friend. What are the odds that she put up a fight or refused to do what they wanted?"

Doug gave a short bark of laughter. "Very high. She is stubborn and would refuse. It's likely the beating was stopped because that wouldn't make her give in. There is almost nothing that would."

"What would?"

Doug shrugged as he thought about it. "We've been friends since we were about two. I can't think of anything really, other than maybe her family or close friends, that would make her give in, and that would really have to be pushed."

Sue nodded. "That's the impression I'm picking up. I want to meet this lady when she's free."

Chapter 17

Matt paced the living room of the safe house. He knew it as they had used it for security purposes before. He just never thought he would be the one using it to stay safe. Ian and Joseph were with him, Joseph patrolling the outside. He could hear Ian in the kitchen, likely getting them something to eat, but he didn't feel like eating. He just wanted to know Sarah was safe.

Ian stopped at the kitchen door and watched his friend, seeing the changes the past few days and weeks had brought to him. There was a hardness in his face that hadn't been there before, even given some of the work they had done. He was beyond the point of simple exhaustion and fatigue and seemed to be holding himself together just by pure adrenalin. He hoped they found Sarah soon, and alive and well. He wasn't sure how Matt would take it otherwise.

Joseph came in through the kitchen. "All okay out there for now. I'll go back out in about an hour." He nodded at the living room. "How is he?"

Ian had turned as Joseph came in. "He's hurting in so many ways, Joseph. I don't think I have ever seen someone hurt like this."

Joseph peered around him at Matt. "He is. He has years of hurt to heal and now this with Sarah. All we can do is pray for them both and support him as much as he will let us.”

Sarah finally roused at the light touch on her shoulder. There was only the light from the moon coming into the room. She had not closed the curtains, needing to feel the openness from the outdoors.

“Sarah, come. We need to leave.” Spence was holding her shoes. “I need to get you out of here tonight.” He reached for her hand and pulled her to her feet, bracing her as she got her balance. “When we leave, don’t say a word.”

Sarah squinted at him, trying to focus. “We’re leaving?”

“Yes. Now shhh, we have to be very quiet.”

Catching her hand, he led her out of the room, stopping to lock it up again, then down the back stairs, through the kitchen, and out the back door. He gently shoved her into a deck chair and knelt to slip on her shoes. With a finger to his lips, he caught her hand again. They made their way across the yard and out to the road. A car was waiting and Spence shoved her into the passenger seat and climbed in the back seat behind her. Bewildered, she was unable to take in what was going on, and couldn’t make out what the two men were talking about.

“Sarah.” She could hear Spence calling her. “Sarah. I need you to wake up, please. We’re here. We’re safe.”

She opened pain-filled eyes and blinked at him. “We’re safe? Where are we?”

“Can you stand?” He ignored her questions and lifted her to feet, moving her away from the car so he could close the door. The car moved off and she turned to watch, swaying and unable to keep her balance. Spence caught her up in his arms and headed for the door of the building. Yes, he thought. This is the right thing to do. It's time for me to leave there.

The desk officer looked up as Spence pushed the door open, then took a second look at the woman in his arms. A shout, and Caleb and Eddie came running from the back. Spence was led to Caleb's office and gently laid Sarah on the couch. He could hear the commotion outside the door and the calls for the paramedics.

Caleb stood back and watched as the paramedics tended to Sarah. He winced as the light shone on her face. How had she survived or did it really look worse than it was?

He turned to study Spence. The man, Caleb figured him to be in his late forties/early fifties, stood as well and watched Sarah. There was something here, Caleb thought, something that needs to be addressed at some point. He made a note to himself to talk with Spence.

The senior paramedic stood and walked over to Caleb. Keeping his voice low, he spoke. "Whoever worked her over is a professional, in my opinion. She's likely got a concussion and she's really tender around the ribs. We'll be transporting shortly."

"Has she roused at all?"

The paramedic shook his head. "No, and that concerns me. The man who brought her in said he had trouble rousing her to get her out of the house and even more trouble rousing her when they got here."

"All right. I'll send officers with you when you go. I want someone with her at all times. In fact, I have one who I want to send with you." He turned to Eddie. "Go find Sue. She can ride with Sarah."

Sue tapped at Caleb's door, and he stepped away from the office to speak with her.

"We have Sarah, Sue. Someone brought her in. I'm getting ready to send officers with her, and you had mentioned you wanted to meet her. Would you go with her and provide security for the night at least?"

Sue looked at him, then glanced through the door where she could see them readying the stretcher to roll out to the ambulance. "Really? How?" She shook her hands. "Never mind. I'll get the details later. I'm in. Let me get my stuff and I'll gladly go."

Eddie spoke from beside him. "Spence, he says his name is, hasn't spoken much. He's what you would call a gentleman's gentleman, has worked there for about three years. He was ready to get out but wanted to make sure Sarah was safe. He says he'll tell his story but only when he knows Sarah is safe and hidden away. Knowing Sarah, that won't happen."

Caleb shook his head. "I agree. I'll go speak with him. Maybe I'll have some luck. You should go find John."

"Already done. He'll be at the hospital when she gets there."

Chapter 18

Abe softly closed the door behind him and sniffed. Ian had been cooking, soup by the aroma, and he couldn't wait to dig into it. Ian was an excellent cook. He dropped his jacket on the back of a chair and looked around.

"Where's Matt?"

"We finally got him to go lay down about four hours ago. I'm not sure if he's slept or not. He can't go on like this, Abe. He's burning out." Ian looked up from the sandwiches he was placing on a plate, and stopped. "You have news?"

Abe nodded, a grim look to his face and hardness in his eyes. Ian studied him, not having seen that strong a combination in Abe before.

"Joseph's on his way in. Why don't you go get Matt?"

Ian didn't move. "All I can ask is, is she alive? I don't want to be the one to tell him she's not."

"She is. Go. Go get Matt."

Matt scrubbed his face as he sat on the side of the bed. Ian stood watching. "I need a shower and a shave, Ian. Can Abe wait?"

"I'm sure he can. Go get cleaned up. There's soup and sandwiches waiting when you're done."

Feeling cleaner and more like himself but still groggy from lack of sleep, Matt slumped into a chair in the kitchen and stared at the bowl of soup Ian placed in front of him. He really didn't feel like eating but knew he needed to. He picked up his spoon and then hesitated, spoonful of soup inches from his mouth. He looked at Abe.

"You're here. Why?"

Abe gave a grim smile. "Eat, then we talk."

Matt narrowed his eyes at Abe, then nodded. He ate what he could and then shoved back his bowl.

"Talk to me, Abe. What's going on?"

Abe cradled his cup of coffee in his hand and rubbed his thumb around the rim. How was he to proceed without Matt running from the room and taking off for the hospital? He caught a subtle movement from Joseph and grinned to himself as Joseph held up the vehicle keys. They were on the same page as to what Matt might try.

"I have news, Matt." Abe kept his eyes on Matt, assessing him. "Caleb has Sarah."

Matt's eyes slid shut in relief. Thank you, Lord, You've brought her back. Then they popped back open. "She's alive, isn't she?"

Abe nodded. "She is. She's at the hospital right now under heavy guard. No one gets near her, not even family right now, and that includes not even John or Doug."

"How did she get away?" The quiet question came from Ian.

"Now, that's a story in itself." Abe leaned

back, draping an arm over the back of his chair. "Apparently, she made a friend while captive, and Spence was able to get her away. He's the one who was responsible for her care and had the only key to the room she was imprisoned in. He just walked out with her during the night."

Matt choked on his sandwich. "He just walked out with her, just like that? No one tried to stop them?"

Abe shook his head. "You could say God was in that. Spence took opportunity of there just being the cook and himself in the house last night and got Sarah out." Abe stopped there, not wanting to continue with what Spence had told them. If he hadn't got her away last night, she would have been dead by noon. The man had no further use for her.

"So no one gets to see her?" Matt sounded hopefully.

"No, not right now." Abe looked at the wall behind Matt, not taking in anything that was hanging there. "The doctors need to evaluate her condition and they were still running some tests when I spoke with Doug early this morning. He'll keep us updated. His concern was that you would break your safety net and try to get to her."

Matt gave a sheepish smile. "That's likely what I would have done."

Abe sighed. "Matt, how many people have we worked security for? You know what we do and why we do it. This time, one of us is the security subject, that would be you. You need to let us do our job, keep you safe, and help catch this guy. Once he finds out Sarah and Spence are gone, all cards are off the table and he is going to come looking for both of you, because both of you can identify him."

Matt stared at his team leader and friend. "I know in my head what you're saying but this time, my heart is involved, and that makes it much more difficult. I just want to see her to make sure she's okay."

"From what Caleb said, you don't want to see her." A grimmer look came down on Abe's face.

Matt blanched at his words, and Ian and Joseph shared a stern look.

Abe nodded. "From what I gather that Spence has said, the driver is a professional and he's the one who worked Sarah over. It's not pretty."

Matt shoved himself away from the table and they heard his bedroom door slam. The three looked at each other. They somehow had to keep him here and away from Sarah, at least until they could figure out how to keep them safe together.

Doug stood looking out at the twilight sky through the window in Sarah's room. John sat at her bedside, dividing his attention between Doug and Sarah. They were close friends, he thought, close enough to be brother and sister.

"What did you say to Tom to make him leave?" John's quiet question caught Doug off guard, and he waited to compose his features before he turned.

Doug shrugged. "He pretty much just told me he was leaving. He didn't want her any more."

John stared at him. "What? Did he really say

that?"

Doug nodded, a hard look in his eyes as he remembered that day. "I could have lost my job over it, certainly my position on the ETF, but it was Sarah he was talking about."

"What exactly did he say?"

Doug shook his head and glanced at Sarah, making sure she was still asleep. He jerked his head towards the hallway and John followed him. They walked down toward the waiting room, where they found an empty area to sit in.

"What did he say?" John repeated his question.

"You really want to know what that scumbag said?"

"Doug! I've never heard you describe anyone like that, not even the ones you've arrested."

Doug shrugged. "It's what he is. You would have slugged him to. His words to me went along the lines of: she's damaged goods now, and with her scars, I don't want my children raised by someone who's disfugured."

John sat back, mouth open, as he took in what Doug had said. "Damaged goods? Disfigured? Is he for real?"

Doug nodded, an unreadable look coming over his face. "I hate to see what happens if he marries and his wife ends up with scars."

"He didn't know her well enough to see beyond the physical to her character. His loss." John smiled. "I wish I had been the one to flatten him."

"Caleb wasn't too happy when he found out a

couple of weeks ago, but there's nothing that can be done now. Tom won't be back in town, he knows better."

"Matt'll be good for her. He's going to bring out something no one else has been able to."

"I know. She has already let him through her defences, and she never does that so quickly."

John stood and moved to stare down the hall to his cousin's room. "Meg and her mom will be back tomorrow. I know Meg will want to come see her, but I don't think Caleb is going to let anyone too close to her."

Doug stood and walked back down the hall, saying over his shoulder, "No, he's not. Matt will try and somehow I think he'll get through."

Chapter 19

Matt paced the living room once again. They weren't letting him outside and he was getting antsy. He needed to be doing something. Ian stood in the kitchen, watching. Matt was getting ready to do something, and he was sure that something would be to run. He knew better but Ian knew Matt was thinking more with his heart than his head. It might come to him setting him down and handcuffing him to a chair to make him stay.

"Don't try it, Matt."

Matt stopped pacing and stood, back rigid and uncompromising. "I know, Ian. I'm just not used to being on this side." He turned. "So how do they do it? The ones we guard? How do they get through these kind of days?"

Ian shrugged. "They all have their ways. Get your Bible and spend time in it. You still have a lot coming up and you need that strength."

The man stared at his driver. "What do you mean, they're gone? We were away for only a day and a night, and they managed to go? How? Who helped him?"

"There's no one left here. Even the cook has gone. Your cleaner refuses to come back." The driver watched as his words sunk it.

The man spun and headed for his study. "Bring

the car around. We'll be leaving for Oak City and find a hotel there to stay in." He paused. "We're not done here. We'll be back once I find out where those two are. No one gets away from me."

Caleb turned from the computer monitor he had been studying as Frankie stopped beside him.

"I spoke with Ben last night. They're home."

Caleb nodded. "What did he have to say?"

"He said he'd think about what I told him and that he'd be in today. He's agreed to work as a consultant on this case."

Caleb felt relief. Ben was good and had insights into town life that few of his officers had. He had agreed with him when he wanted to retire, but he missed him.

"Has Abe called?"

Caleb studied the monitor again as he spoke, "He did. Matt took it hard. Abe figures they're going to have a time trying to keep him in the safe house, unless someone can get through to him." He turned to Frankie again. "How is it going with Spence?"

"He's a fountain of information even though he didn't work there that long. Our people can't keep up with him. I still think it's bigger than just Matt."

"Why do you say that?"

Eddie shrugged. "I don't know. I can feel the evil, just like before, but this time, there's a difference to it, a largeness we've never seen before. And I think Abe is the target, and whoever it is, he is using Matt to get to Abe."

Before they could continue their conversation, a

call came in for Caleb and by the time he was finished, Frankie had moved on.

Sarah stirred, her head turning restlessly on the pillow. She cracked her eyes open. The headache wasn't as bad today as it had been. She didn't remember a headache like that ever in her life. Movement came to her right and she cautiously turned her head to look. A woman stood there, a police officer she guessed, given the weapon and badge on her belt.

"Hi, Sarah, I'm Sue."

Sarah tried to moisten dry lips but her mouth was dry. Sue smiled and then helped her raise up enough to have a drink.

"Where am I?"

"You're in the hospital, Sarah. I'm a friend staying with you for a couple of days."

Sarah's forehead settled into a frown. "Why do I need a friend staying with me?"

Sue caught the uncertain look in Sarah's eyes. "You don't remember anything of the last few days."

Sarah went to shake her head but instead spoke. "No, I don't. Why am I here?"

"You had an incident, Sarah, and ended up with a concussion. The doctors wanted you to stay in the hospital for a couple of days until they could assess you completely."

"An incident? What kind of incident?"

"We'll explain it when you're thinking clearer. Right now, the doctors want you to rest as much as you can."

Sarah sank back in relief. "What day is it?" When told, she continued, "I don't remember anything past being at the construction site with Joseph. Joseph! Is he all right?"

"He is, Sarah, just worried about you."

"What about Matt? Is he okay?"

"He is. He wants to come see you, but Caleb isn't letting anyone in right now, other than John and Doug, and that's only because they have your medical power of attorney."

Sarah sighed as she drifted off, "Tell Caleb I want to see Matt. If he doesn't let him come, I'm going to go find him."

Sue smiled as she listened to Sarah. Frankie was right. Those two were in love. She looked up at the ceiling. God, I don't know if You even exist. I've never believed in You, but if You do, please please keep these two safe.

The man listened as he was briefed. They had found Matt. Sarah he already knew was in the hospital and closely guarded. That was all right. He had no further use for her. When the time was right, she would die.

He turned his thoughts as to how to get to Matt. It would be difficult, but not impossible. Nothing was impossible if he put out enough money, and how he resented having to put out more money. His people had failed him. The rage was building inside him, and it had to have an outlet and soon. Matt was his outlet. He needed to get to him and destroy him. As far as he was concerned, Matt had destroyed him.

Caleb tapped at the hospital room door and

waited for Sue to answer. As he stepped in, his gaze went to Sarah, and he winced afresh at the vivid colouring on her face.

"How is she?"

"The doctors said other than a concussion and some bruised ribs, she fine. They are concerned about the hip she broke a few years ago, though. They want to do some more imagaing tomorrow."

"Has she been awake?"

Sue nodded as she turned to watch Sarah. "She has. You won't like it. She can't remember anything that happened. The last she remembers is being on the job site with Joseph."

Caleb sighed. "That's about what I figured you'd say. We'll just have to work around it."

Sue smiled. "She did have a message for you, though."

Caleb turned a puzzled glance to Sue. "She can't remember anything about what happened, but she has a message for me?"

Sue nodded. "She wants to see Matt. If you don't bring him to her, she's going to go and find him."

Caleb gave a soft laugh. "That's what Abe's getting too. Ian has Matt pretty much settled down now. Let's not tell him who Sarah has asked for."

"Caleb." They turned at the soft voice from the bed.

Caleb moved to stand beside her. "Sarah. Hi."

"Caleb, don't let him hurt anyone else. I

couldn't stop him." Sarah's eyes filled with tears. "I wouldn't beg him to stop, so he just kept hitting me. That man just let him."

Caleb reached to wipe tears from her face. "I know, Sarah, I know. Spence has given us names. We're looking for them."

Sarah gave him a puzzled look. "Who's Spence?"

Caleb's eyes met Sue's and he knew what she meant. "A friend, Sarah, someone who was a really good friend to you."

"Thank him for me." Her voice drifted off as she fell back asleep.

Caleb's face settled into a hard mask. "We need to catch this guy, Sue. If she says anything at all, call me."

"I will, Caleb."

Chapter 20

Caleb tracked Abe down in his office at Rebel's. He sank down into the easy chair and gratefully took the cup of tea he was handed.

Abe studied him. This was getting to him. He was tired and he needed to be home with his wife and boys. Lord, please let this end and soon.

"It's getting to you, Caleb. You need to go spend time with Hannah."

Caleb nodded. "I know. This time, she hasn't come up with a name. I'm just as glad. It takes so much out of her when she does."

"Where are we standing with Matt?"

"We still haven't found the man. We have tracked him to a hotel in Oak City but he's already checked out of there. Oak City police are looking for him as well."

"We'll find him. Hopefully soon." Abe sat back, and folded his hands across his abdomen. "How's Sarah?"

Caleb shook his head. "She really doesn't have a memory of what happened, other than that she was beaten and couldn't stop it. She doesn't remember much else. She doesn't even remember who Spence is."

"That's understandable. I hear tell she

threatened to go find Matt."

"She did, and she probably will too. I'll leave the security up to you. We'll have to put it on Sarah now as well. I have a female officer with her, one of my detectives, and I would like her to stay with her if possible. Sue's agreeable."

"I'll let you know. We'll be moving Matt anyway. I have a feeling that safe house has been found."

Ian went to find Joseph. "We're moving. Abe has word from the street this house has been found."

"How?"

"Abe doesn't know yet. He has Murphy working on that. He wants to move Matt somewhere we can watch both him and Sarah. Caleb thinks she'll be released in the next day or so, and it will be easier to keep them together. By the way, Caleb is insisting on of his female detectives join us this time, for Sarah's sake."

Joseph thought about it. "I don't like it, bringing in an unknown, but I can see why he would want that."

"Abe's on his way in now. He expects to be here in about 15 minutes."

"Did he say where we were headed?"

Ian shook his head. "No, he didn't. He and Murphy will have come up with a place."

Matt turned as Abe stopped behind him. "Where to now, Abe?"

Abe studied Matt, seeing the fatigue in his face and eyes. They were all tired, and fighting to find the man responsible was wearing them down. "We're going somewhere we can keep you and Sarah together. It doesn't make sense to split you two up."

Matt's eyes slid shut in relief. "Thank you, Abe. I have been praying that you would do this."

Abe was amused. "So you think your prayers did this, do you?"

Matt smiled. "Of course, else you wouldn't have done it."

Abe shook his head. "Come on, let's get on the road. I'll take you to your girl."

"Now, wait a minute. Who said she was my girl?"

The three men surrounding him spoke in a chorus. "We all do."

"Sarah, can you wake up for me?"

Sarah stirred as she heard a voice now grown familiar. "I'm awake, doctor. Now what test do you have for me?"

The physician laughed. "None for right now. We're letting you go We have some gentlemen here who say they've come to spirit you away somewhere."

"I'm too tired. Tell them to come back." Sarah drifted off again.

The physician took a look at her, then at Abe and Murphy standing beside Sue. "I'm sorry. I can't get her to wake up for you."

Abe shook his head. "It's understandable. If you could get a nurse to help Sue get Sarah dressed, then we'll take it from there."

Sue opened the door and beckoned them in. "She's still out. We can't get her to wake up."

Murphy reached to gather her into his arms. "Lead the way, Abe. Sue, you follow."

Abe slid open the door of their van, and then held out his arms for Sarah. Murphy stepped in and reached back for her, settling her into one of the seats and buckling her in. Sue slid in beside Matt, who turned to watch Sarah. Sliding the door closed behind him, Abe buckled himself into the front seat.

Ian pulled away, eyes, though tired, vigilant for a shadow. He could see nothing but he could feel the evil around them.

"I can feel him, Abe, I just can't see him."

"I know. I don't like this."

Murphy carried Sarah into the bedroom they had decided would be hers and laid her gently on the bed. Sue nodded in thanks.

"What do you need for her?" Murphy kept his voice low.

"Some water, ice, and maybe some juice. She prefers orange juice and absolutely refuses apple juice."

"I'll see what we have. Ian's making us some dinner. Come out when you get her settled."

Matt sat at the table, staring at his plate. He was almost too tired to eat.

Sue slid into the chair beside him. "You need to eat, Matt."

He nodded. "How's Sarah?"

"She's still asleep. The doctors said she would be like this for a couple of more days. She is in some pain but we're seeing the pain medications to the minimum. And no, I won't take you to see her if you don't eat."

Ian slid a plate of food in front of her and she thanked him. "This looks good, Ian. How did you manage to get a gourmet meal like this ready so quick?"

Ian gave a quick grin. "I usually have meals done up and frozen. When Abe decided we needed to move Matt and Sarah, he grabbed some of them out of the freezer for me."

She tasted her meal and closed her eyes. "This is so good. I vote you stop doing security and open your own restaurant. I would eat there every night."

"Not happening, Sue." Murphy spoke up. "We need him on the team. Do you want some of that poison you call herbal tea?"

"That would be lovely, mint if you have it."

The men looked between Murphy and Sue.

"We're old friends, Abe." Sue spoke up. "We've known each other since college."

Matt pushed his plate back and turned to Sue "Tell me. Tell me how Sarah really is."

Sue contemplated her plate, fork dangling between her thumb and forefinger. She pushed her plate away, laying the fork on it, knowing she had eaten all she could.

"Sarah is recovering, Matt. She took a beating

and the man, Spence said he was the driver or chauffeur, is the one who did it. Whoever he is, he's a professional. She's battered, she's bruised, she has some pretty sore ribs, a black eye."

She turned to look at him as his face stiffened. "No, don't go there. Let it rest."

He turned to look at her.

"You tell me you're a Christian. I'm trying to understand why your God allows this to happen. Sarah has been able to say a few words to me. I kind of get what she's staying but I still don't understand.

"Now back to Sarah. You are aware there were two videos sent it?" When Matt shook his head, she sighed, then continued. "Okay, so we need to go back a few days. Eddie received two different videos of Sarah. In one, she was able to send a message to Doug. The second video we figured out was made the same day, but was dated to the next day. No, you're never going to see those videos. They're sealed into evidence."

Abe spoke up. "So what happens now, Sue, from your investigative point of view?"

"They're still working on the videos and the text messages. They're pinning down the dates and locations. Spence gave the address and Caleb was able to get warrants. A team is working through the house now, but it will take a few days."

She looked around at the men seated at the table, her gaze narrowing on Matt. His eyes were on his plate and it looked as if he was barely hanging on. She looked up as Ian moved to Matt's side, hauled him to his feet and then steered him down the hall to his bedroom.

Abe stared after them, then looked back at Sue. "There's one thing I don't understand, Sue. Sarah shouldn't be this groggy. After this amount of time, she should be more alert."

Sue nodded. "I agree. I have cut back on her pain meds as she does seem to be in pain, but there was the other medication the doctor insisted she needed." Sue was on her feet, moving towards the bedroom as she spoke. She was back with the bottle i her hand. "Here. I'm not familiar with medications."

Abe took it, read it, and then handed it to Ian. "How often was she to get this?"

Sue thought about what the instructions were that she had been given. "He said every four hours but I haven't been. Why? What is it?"

"It's a sedative and can be highly addictive if used wrong. I can't tell from the look of the tablets if they're what the label says they are. We need to get this to Caleb." Abe's eyes narrowed. "What did you bring with you from the hospital? Go get it."

Sue's eyes flickered to his and she nodded. "Of course. He couldn't get into her but the health care team could." She was once again on her feet, meeting Ian in the hallway.

She spread out what she had brought from the hospital on the kitchen table, not a lot really, but enough that a tracking device could have easily been hidden. Ian sorted through the medication bottles, then turned his attention to the clothing. He felt along the seams of her jacket and stopped.

Abe handed him his pocketknife. Making a

quick, careful slice into the fabric, Ian pulled out a small tracking device. He held it up with a grim look on his face.

Abe stood back. "We've been compromised. Murphy, call Caleb. Let him know. We're going to have to move again. I'm hoping we can get by until morning, just for Matt and Sarah's sake, but I think we're going to have to move tonight."

"Ian, Murphy, go over everything that was brought in. If we have to leave things here, we will. Sue, you know what we're looking for now. Check the clothes Sarah has on. Does she have any bandages on or stitches?" When Sue shook her head, he nodded. "Good. Now we don't have to remove stitches."

Abe turned as his phone vibrated and walked away to answer it. When he returned, new plans had been made. He sent Joseph to make sure the vehicles were ready and to watch the roads.

Sue entered the kitchen, her hand outstretched. She had found another device. She shook her head.

"How did they manage this when I was with her?"

"It is surprising how quickly they can work. Caleb is going to have all the medical staff interviewed, but he suspects the doctor is the one we're looking at. He hasn't been able to track him down yet."

"And I doubt he will, not from what I know."

They turned as Matt came into the kitchen. Even though he had only had about an hour's sleep, he was alert.

"What's going on, Abe?" Matt noted the grim look on the faces around him. His eyes slid shut and then opened. "Not again."

Abe nodded. "Someone at the hospital. Matt, I need to you take a look at Sarah." He handed him the sedative bottle. "Sue was told to give her these every four hours. She hasn't been."

Matt took a look and then nodded. "That would explain why she's like she is." He turned, Sue on his heels, and headed for Sarah.

Chapter 21

"Caleb, we're heading back to Rebel's." Abe stood in the garage, waiting for Joseph to come back and report. "We're going to split up into the vehicles and head out in different ways."

"Are you sure this will work?"

Abe gave a short bark of laughter. "Has anything worked out yet? How's the investigation coming?"

"It's coming. Ben's in here now and is helping to sort through names."

"Good. He knows so many people and their connections, that will help." He turned as Joseph came in and nodded. "We're set to go in about 15 minutes. You're set from your end?"

"We are. Give me a head's up when you leave."

Abe pocketed his phone. "Let's go, Joseph. We're not taking anything with us. We can come back for it later. The guys are ready for us at Rebel's?"

"They are. Peter sent over some of his people as well. Amy's waiting to spell off with Sue."

Abe nodded and headed into the house. He had planned to separate Matt and Sarah but then decided not to.

They headed out at the same time, separating into the three vehicles and going different directions. This, Abe hoped, would help to confuse the followers. Caleb's men moved in, their vehicles a close match to his, adding to the mix.

"What do you mean, they're gone from there and you have no idea where they are?" The man's face was reddening from anger and he was shaking in his rage. "I thought you had it arranged so that we never lost track of them."

"I did. I have no idea how they found out."

"Find them. I need to get rid of him and soon."

The driver stared at his employer and then turned and walked from the room. He stopped, turned and stared back at the closed door. They were in a house not too many people knew the man owned. He suddenly felt dirty and ashamed. How had his life got to this point? He turned again, headed for the door, and walked out, walked away from the man who had owned him in body but not in soul. He was done. He walked away from the house, down to the road, and kept going. He knew he wouldn't be able to hide from his employer for long or from those over him, but he would do his best. He headed back into town, catching the town bus as it slowed and stopped beside him. He stood on the steps of the police department, studied the building, took a deep breath, and then went in.

Caleb turned as Eddie entered his office and closed the door.

"What is it, Eddie?" Caleb eyed the remaining

paperwork on his desk. He had gotten through most of it, other than the budget allocations, but that would have to wait.

"You won't believe this, but the man's driver, chauffeur, whatever you want to call him, just walked in and gave himself up."

Caleb sat back, stunned. "He just walked in on his own? We didn't have to go find him?" As Eddie shook his head, Caleb sat forward again. "What's his story?"

"I'm just going to go in and interview him, but he said he has felt guilty since Sarah. There was something about her that disturbed him. And when he was told today that Matt would have to die, something changed inside him. He can't do that kind of work any more."

Caleb stood. "All right. Let's go see what he has to say."

Sarah stirred, her mind feeling clear for the first time in days. She sat up, ready to face her day once again. There was some pain, but not as much as she had expected. She looked around, not sure where she was, but she figured Abe had her stuck somewhere safe. She headed for the bathroom. A shower sounded wonderful, and she so needed to wash her hair. She gave a squeak as she saw her face. No wonder it felt tender.

She searched the countertop and saw the makeup someone had thoughtfully provided. She seldom used it but today she would. It would help to cover some of the garishness of her bruises.

She stopped at the kitchen doorway. Sue sat at

the table, a newspaper open in front of her. She didn't know the other woman who sat there. They looked up as she hesitated and smiled.

"Sarah." Sue spoke. "It is so good to see you up on your feet. I was beginning to wonder if we would. This is Amy. She's here for a few days of rest and relaxation, she says. Abe figured we three females would like to bunk together."

"We're at Abe's?" Sarah moved to the counter and poured a cup of coffee, then turned, leaning back on the counter. She twisted the cup in her hands, not sure what was going on any more.

"We are. We found a tracking device in some of your stuff and Abe moved us." Sue stood and moved to the counter. "What do you feel like eating?"

"Just some toast, Sue. I can get it."

Sue shook her head. "Sit. I've got it. You'll need a day or so longer to let the headaches settle."

Abe met with the team in the conference room. "Caleb just called. The driver walked in and gave himself up. Somehow, Sarah reached him through to him." He turned his eyes to Matt. "He also said there's a price on Matt's head. The man wants you dead, Matt."

Matt sat back, his face paling. "I knew he was mean, but I just never expected that."

"We're going to do our best to see that doesn't happen. We have that assignment we have to go on at the end of this week. Matt, is your head in place enough you're with us?"

Matt stared at Abe, then looked around at his team members. He didn't want to put them at risk, but he also didn't want to let them down. "With God's help, I'm in."

Abe went over the specifics of the assignment, then stopped. He studied each of the men sitting there, each with their own personalities, their own gifts, yet united together as a team. "Team up with a buddy, guys. Spend time each day in prayer. We're going to need it this time like we have never before."

He stood on the rocks above the compound and watched. It was up to him now, everyone else had let him down. Somehow he had to get to him and it wouldn't be easy. He had tried with the girlfriend, that didn't work. He knew it wouldn't work with his mother, he had tried that in the past. So how? Pressure was bearing down on him from above and he needed to solve this problem.

Chapter 22

Caleb turned as Matt walked towards him across the parking lot. He raised his eyes but didn't see anyone with him.

"Matt, where's your team?"

"Murphy's in the vehicle right behind you. I needed to talk to you and I didn't think coming in to your office was a good idea."

Caleb studied him. "What about?"

"I want this to end. We're away on assignment at the end of the week but when we're back, I want to go on the aggressive. I want to lure him out and meet with him. It's the only way it will stop. You'll have about a week to come up with a plan. If you don't, I'll go it alone." Matt walked past Caleb, leaving Caleb staring after him.

Caleb shook his head as Murphy drove away, then went to find Eddie and Frankie. If Matt was serious, they had planning to do.

"Are you really ready to do that, Matt?" Murphy wasn't questioning the reason, just if it was what Matt really wanted to do.

Matt nodded. "He's controlled my life for years. I need to put it to rest. You know how you are always talking about forgiveness? I need to meet with him to work out how to forgive him."

Murphy thought about that. Matt was right. He did need this meeting.

Sarah had gone back to her own home. She was tired of being caged. She felt like she was in a holding pattern and she didn't like that at all.

Hearing the doorbell from the kitchen, she padded her way through in her bare feet. She wasn't expecting anyone. Peeking out the front room window, she saw a delivery waiting for her. Strange, she thought. I wasn't waiting for any delivery. She waited. The delivery van had left, pulling in next door and the courier heading for their door. She cracked open her door a bit and again studied the package. This is ridiculous, she thought. All I have to do is step out and look at it. I don't have to pick it up or bring it in.

She stepped out onto the porch, scanning the area. It looked clear, but she could feel that sense of evil again. She bent to look at the label and felt hands on her, arms pinning hers, and a cloth across her mouth. Struggling in vain, she was lifted and carried to the delivery van and shoved inside. A hood came down over her head and she felt her wrists and ankles being bound. Lord, where are you? I can't do this again.

Doug slowed as he passed Sarah's house. That was strange, he thought, the cats are outside and her door is wide open. That never happens. Throwing his vehicle into park, he ran for her home, slowing as he approached. His phone out, he made the call to dispatch, asking for backup. His gut was telling him Sarah was in trouble.

He cornered Spider and Miss Muffet and locked

them in his house, then came back. With his backup in place, they searched the house. Sarah was missing. Doug stepped back onto the porch. Where was she? And how? There was no clue as to where she was. Even the package had disappeared.

Murphy slowed as he approached Sarah's. Matt had insisted they come and kept telling Murphy Sarah was in trouble. They just gotten back to town that morning and Murphy really didn't want to be driving through town, but he knew Matt would do the same for him. His heart sank as he saw the activity going on at Sarah's.

Matt was out of the truck almost before it had stopped. Doug was leaning against a cruiser, hands jammed into his jeans' pockets, feet crossed at the ankles. Murphy handed him an extra jacket and he shrugged into it.

"What happened, Doug?"

Doug shrugged, eyes not leaving the front door. "I got home, noticed Sarah's door open and the cats outside and came over. We've searched. She's not there."

Matt slumped against the car. His instinct had been right. Sarah was gone but who had her.

Caleb approached them, a grimmer look on his face than Doug could remember seeing in recent years. He handed Doug his phone.

Doug scanned the text, then his eyes shot to Caleb's. "He has her again?"

Caleb nodded. "A trade this time isn't in the works. He wants Matt to meet him, but he's not giving up Sarah."

"That's not good." Doug looked up at Caleb. "Now what."

"Now, we take Matt with us, and start planning. Abe and the rest of them are on their way in. ETF details are yours but I think they might be able to give some input. They'll be backing you if needed."

Caleb looked past Matt at Murphy and nodded at Matt. Murphy tugged him back to the vehicle, Matt almost dragging his heels.

"Let's go, Matt. We're meeting at the department. We have planning to do."

Matt turned to him, a hard look in his eyes, and a stern set to his face unlike him. "I want to trade for her."

"That's not happening, Matt. He's not trading this time."

Matt was silent during the drive and while they were waiting. The eyes of the men with him watched him on and off, knowing that at the slightest chance, he would be gone and off on his own to find her.

Plans made as best they could, it was now a waiting game. Their prayer was that Sarah was still alive and that they could get both of them out when the opportunity presented itself.

Sarah stirred, turning her head to look around. Her eyes slid closed. Please, Lord, not again. I just can't go through another beating. A sound at the door had her on her feet, facing it from the opposite side of the bed.

He entered and stared at her, not saying a word. Then he spoke. "You'll not get away again, my dear.

This time, I will keep you."

Her chin lifting in defiance, Sarah refused to speak to him.

"Not saying anything? You will soon enough." He turned and left, locking the door behind him.

Sarah stood for a moment, listening, then began a systemic search of the room, for anything she could use as a weapon or to help her get away. This time, she wouldn't have Spence's help.

Chapter 23

Where was she? That was the question each man gathered around the conference table was asking. The investigation was ongoing but he had hidden his tracks well. They weren't able to pinpoint him to any particular place.

Eddie walked in with Ben. "I think we've narrowed down where he is. Between Spence and the driver, and Ben's memory, we've got a location for him."

Caleb's phone interpreted them. "Logan." His eyes sought for the computer techs and motioned for them to try and trace the call. If he could keep him on the line long enough, that was.

"I want Matt. He is to come, alone, to this address. Don't try and wire him. He will be searched."

The phone clicked off and Caleb knew they hadn't had enough time to trace the call. His eyes searched each of the men who were waiting for him to speak.

"He's given us an address and a time frame for when to be there. He has also said no wires, that Matt would be searched. What do we have that we can use? Abe, do you have something?"

Joseph was up and out of the room before Caleb had finished speaking.

"Joseph's on his way to get something. It should work."

Joseph handed Matt the device. "It's working, I tested it. If you have to, pass it on to Sarah. It will work for either one of you."

"Thanks, Joseph."

Matt walked away from the van, leaving Murphy and Ian watching him and praying for his safety and that of Sarah.

"I don't like this, Ian." Murphy's brows were drawn into a frown. "It's too easy."

"I know. I feel like we're puppets being yanked around. Is the tracker working?"

"Joseph says it is. Even searching him, they shouldn't find it."

Matt stood at the phone booth he had been directed to, looking around. The phone rang and he answered, not saying anything. He turned and walked back past the van and towards the bus station. Once inside the station, he walked through and out the employee's entrance. The man waiting there just pointed to the van. Matt hesitated and felt the shove from behind. Okay, so he means business. As long as he could keep his head on straight and think, maybe there was a way for him to get Sarah away.

Sarah heard the door open and turned to look. It was someone different this time, tall, heavyset. He frowned as he stared at her.

"He was specific. You were to dress for dinner."

Sarah's chin tilted. "Sorry, I only dress up for

dinner with friends, and I don't consider him a friend."

A glint of admiration came into the man's eyes and was quickly extinguished. Sarah wondered at that, then followed as he motioned her from the room. She was led to the massive dining room and seated at the table. She looked around. The table was set for three. Okay, she thought, I doubt that guy would be joining us. He doesn't look the type. Who is?

The older man stopped as he spotted her. Rage swept through him. How dare she not follow his instructions. They had been clear. She was to dress in the wardrobe provided.

She watched him and saw how he tried to control his rage, not quite succeeding. Good. He's rattled, not so in control any more.

"You were to dress for dinner. Why haven't you?"

"I told your man, I only dress for dinner with friends. I don't consider you a friend."

She licked at the blood where her tooth had cut her lip. Not a smart move, Sarah, getting him agitated so early. The mark showed red against her pale skin. She watched as he seated himself at the head of the table and waited. Hearing footsteps behind her, she watched his face and saw the self satisfied look, almost triumphant look come across his face. She shivered at the evil she felt. Lord, we need You here. Protect us. Send us those angels to surround us.

She looked up and saw Matt standing across from her before sliding into the chair. A split second look at him and she drew from deep within her to keep her face impassive.

"I believe you know Matt, don't you, my dear?"

"Sorry, I'm not your dear and dislike being called that. I think I vaguely remember meeting Matt at some time or other."

A heavy fist slamming onto the table made the silverware and dishes jump, almost causing the water to spill from the glasses. Matt jerked and then stared at Sarah. She was sitting there, calm and peaceful, the noise not seeming to have affected her.

"You know him and he knows you. Don't give me that."

"Give you what? I don't discuss who or who may not be known to me with strangers."

Matt couldn't believe he was hearing her bait him. Wrong move, Sarah. He'll chew you up and spit you out.

"I'm not a stranger to Matt, and neither are you. That means we're not strangers."

"Sorry, buddy, but it does. I don't really recall my last meeting with you, but I know it was very unpleasant. People like you don't belong with my friends."

Rage turned his face almost purple. He struggled to control it as the first course was set in front on them. Sarah studied hers and then looked at Matt. He was staring down at his plate, no expression on his face.

"Eat." They were commanded.

Matt reluctantly picked up his fork and tried to

eat, but eventually laid it back down. Sarah made no such pretence, simply sitting there, hands folded in her lap.

"I said, eat."

Sarah shook her head. "No, I don't think so. I know you like to play with sedations, so unless you can guarantee me that this food isn't drugged, I'm not touching it."

Joseph was listening in on the conversation and choked back laughter as he listened to her. The tracker also had the ability to transfer conversation. He put the audio on speaker and the men just shook their heads.

"She's baiting him, Caleb," Eddie muttered. "What is she hoping to gain?"

"She may be baiting him, but she's also keeping them alive. As long as he has an opponent he considers worthy, he won't kill them."

"Not yet, but you can bet that's in the plans." Eddie turned to search the room. "Ben had an interesting take on what's going on. Have you taken to him?"

"I did and I think I agree with him."

"So you think someone here is town, besides Benson, is working with him?"

"I do. I also think we've just seen the tip of the iceberg. I think Abe is the real target, and Matt is being used to get to him."

Eddie turned to him in frustration. "Abe? And Matt is being used? What happens if it doesn't work? Does this guy go on to another one of Abe's team members?"

"I hope we catch him before that happens, but that is always a possibility."

Chapter 24

Matt paced the study they had been taken to after the meal. Sarah sat and watched him. She knew he wanted to talk to her but was playing it safe by ignoring her.

The man entered and then sat behind the massive desk. He pulled out papers from a drawer and studied them. His eyes raised to Matt and watched him pace.

"Sit." Matt turned and watched him in return. "I said sit."

"No, I don't think so." Matt was sure of himself. "You don't control my life any more."

Sarah stared between them, trying to figure out what was going on.

"I said sit!" The man's voice raised.

Matt backed up and leaned against the credenza on the opposite wall. He was not prepared at this time to let this man win.

"Still stubborn and arrogant, I see." He was glared at. "It didn't work for your father either."

Matt didn't rise to the bait. He waited, wondering where this was going. He was stared at for the longest time and he refused to back down.

The man finally waved to his bodyguard in the

door. "Take these to their rooms." His attention returned to them. "If either one of them tries to escape, kill the other one." His head dropped back to the papers he was studying.

Caleb eyes flew to the audio equipment. This man may be crazy but he would be deadly. He turned to Doug.

"What do you think, Doug?"

"It's a tough area to get in close. Provided there are no cameras on the outside, we could try and slip in close tonight and take them. It's easier in the daylight, if we can wait for it."

"Figure it out and let me know. Abe's working with you on it. Get together with your men and come up with a plan." Doug walked away to find Abe. "I wish I knew exactly what he was after. Then we would have a better plan."

A voice came from behind him and he turned. "Hannah, what are you doing here?" He walked towards his wife and drew her aside.

"It's different this time, Caleb. It's not a name, it's a reason." She looked up at him. "Why did God change this?"

Caleb drew his wife into his arms and hugged her tight. "He knows why, favourite girl. He gives us what we need as we need it, and this time it's not a name, it's a why."

Hannah leaned back to look up at him. "I know you're not going to like the why any more than you would a name." She told him, and he agreed with her. He didn't like the why.

He walked her to the door and then sought out his office. He needed to think this one through and pray about it. Ben and Eddie found him a while later, and hesitated about entering. He waved them in.

"Hannah was here." Ben studied Caleb, reading in him what had happened.

"She was. This time, God's changed it. He's given her the why, not the who."

Eddie stilled, then shrugged. "We already know who but the why?"

Caleb told them what Hannah had said, and it stunned them. They looked at each other and then Caleb.

"We've got work to do and very quickly, if this is true."

Matt studied the bedroom he had been assigned and like Sarah, searched for something to use as a weapon. Nothing. He stood, staring around, and then headed for the windows. They opened but it was a long drop to the pavement below. Nothing that he could cling to to escape. And he wouldn't have Sarah with him if he did.

The next morning, Matt and Sarah were ushered to a smaller dining room and again ordered to sit. The man stared at them as they didn't touch their food once again.

He threw his fork down in frustration and shoved back from the table. "Bring them to me in 10 minutes."

Matt grew tense, having a pretty good idea of what was coming. He looked over at Sarah and his eyes stopped. She was at peace and he wished he could talk with her to find out how she was, but they needed to keep up their pretence that they really didn't know each other well. The bodyguard motioned them to move and letting Sarah go first, he followed her out of the room. Sarah was directed to a different chair this time, and the bodyguard stood behind her, hand on her shoulder.

Matt turned to the man and waited. Today would be the day he found out what he had suffered for all those years ago.

The man looked down at the papers he had slapped on the desk and then at Matt. "You're going to sign these papers today, Matt. I have waited for too many years for this."

"I don't understand." Matt was genuinely puzzled.

"You never knew that your father's line went back to an earldom in England, did you? That the title went down to every oldest son and that it could be left to some male in a will. Your grandfather refused to turn that over to me, as did your father. Both of them had to die. Your oldest brother, ditto. Your sister wasn't supposed to be with them that day. She's collateral damage."

Matt could feel the grief and rage building inside him and fought to tamp it down. There was no way he would going to let this man win that way. "So, what you're telling me is that you had my grandfather, father, brother and sister killed? Then you moved in on my grandmother in her grief. When did you find out you wouldn't be the title, that it would come to me?"

"It doesn't go to you. I found out a couple of years ago that with the oldest son's death, the line died out, unless it was passed on by will. You are going to sign this will to give that to me."

Matt stared at him. "What's in it for you, anyway? There's no money. Titles don't mean anything any more?"

"Where I am going, they do."

Matt shook his head. "No, I'm not signing."

The men listening to the audio heard Sarah give a low cry, then her voice came clear. "No, Matt, don't sign it. He's not worth it. If he kills us today, he kills us. He still won't get what he wants if you're dead."

"But if I hurt you, he'll sign." The depravity came through in the man's gruff voice.

"No, he won't." Sarah's voice was calm and low. "I know he won't."

There was silence and then they heard the sound of a struggle.

"Doug, move in." Caleb voice cut through the chatter to Doug.

Matt struggled with the bodyguard for the gun, finally wrested it from him. He pointed it at the man who was his step-grandfather.

"This is over. There is no paperwork to sign. That earldom, it was given up legally by my great-grandfather. There is nothing there now. You killed my family for nothing." He moved to Sarah, pushing her behind him and out the door. "We're leaving."

"Not so fast." The man held up a switch. "I

have just activated a bomb. You won't make it to the door."

Matt caught Sarah's hand ran from the room. He headed for the dining room, knowing the French doors to the outside would be the quickest.

Caleb was frantically calling Doug back. Doug slid to a stop at the door, listened and then waved his men back.

"There's a bomb about to go off. Joseph said Matt's on the move outside the house. Let's go."

They raced away from the building. They could see Matt and Sarah across the lawn, close to the tree line, slower than they were because of Sarah's limitations.

The earth shook and the building collapsed, sending debris flying around them. Doug and his men were flung to the ground from the force of the blast. What had he used? Doug wondered. He turned and his heart sank. He couldn't see either Matt or Sarah, just the field of debris. He picked himself up and ran for where he had last seen them, his men following him and Abe's team running from where they had been standing.

They frantically searched for the two, carefully moving debris. They couldn't find them. How had they disappeared?

Caleb stood, looking around. They had searched the whole area. He knew they had gotten out of the building, he had seen them himself. Where had they gotten to?

Chapter 25

Matt rolled his head to the side and then rolled over onto his back. He hurt all over. His head was aching and when he opened his eyes, he could barely see for the pain. He felt hands on his head but before he could open his eyes all the way, he drifted off again.

Sarah knelt by Matt, feeling once again his face. She had come to, she thought, about thirty minutes ago. She raised her eyes and looked around the room, basement really. No, she thought, not a basement. She stood, waited for her balance to return, then limped to the window. Scrubbing it with the side of her hand, she managed to clear a small area. She couldn't see much, it was dark, but she thought she saw a large building in the distance. Where were they? The last she could remember was Matt grabbing her hand and running through the dining room.

Matt stirred again towards morning. He raised himself up and stared around in the dim light. He could see Sarah curled up near him, asleep. He stood, like she had, and wandered the building, stopping at the same window and wiping a larger area clean. They were near the house they had been in. He could still see the smoke in the air. But how had they gotten from there to here? He could vaguely remember men being beside them and grabbing them.

He had thought it was his team. He searched for the door and tried it. Locked from the outside he thought, but it's flimsy. He could break it down if needed. But who had brought them here?

He knelt by Sarah. She was sound asleep, bruised and battered once again, but alive. He slid down to lean against the wall, as near as he could get to her.

Abe slumped in his chair, exhausted and disheartened. Matt and Sarah had just disappeared. They had searched the area under the debris but hadn't found them.

Caleb slid a cup of coffee towards him across the table and sat, a cup of tea in his own hands. He raised red, sore eyes and searched the room. His men were scattered throughout, the same despair evident that he felt. Doug and the ETF were there as well. His eyes searched and he found Eddie and Frankie working with the investigators, trying to determine what had gone wrong.

"Joseph, did that tracker stop working?"

Joseph nodded. "It was working until the blast, then it stopped. I was praying it would still work."

"Did you try it again today?" Caleb was taking a shot in the dark.

He shook his head, then stood and went to his laptop, bringing up the program. He watched as the program worked, then his hand stilled.

"Abe." At the tone of his voice, all movement stopped in the room. Abe was out of his chair and at his side, Caleb right behind him.

"It's working again. We have a location."

Abe ran from the room, his team with him, Joseph taking time to gather up his phone and bring up the program on it. Caleb followed.

The vehicles stopped, the men exited and watched as Murphy and Ian scouted the area.

"It looks clear, Abe. I don't see anyone. It's a pretty decrepit building, more like a shed, I'd say." Murphy came towards them. "Our concern is that it's boobytrapped in some way."

"Check it out. Nathaniel, Ike, you're on that."

They waited, as hard as it was, for the two men to return.

"Do we know if Matt's by himself or is Sarah there?" Caleb asked.

"I can't tell from the tracker," Joseph said. "It only tracks him."

Ike appeared and waved them forward. "No traps as far as we can tell. This is just so bizarre."

The lock quickly broken off and the door pulled open, Caleb and Abe entered. Neither Matt nor Sarah stirred as they approached them.

"Sarah's got a good pulse. So does Matt. Let's get them out of here. Murphy, need your help." Abe squatted by the two of them and let his eyes scan them. He could see bruises on the arms and faces. Let them be okay, please, Lord.

Caleb gathered Sarah into his arms and stood, walking carefully so as to keep the jarring to a minimum. Murphy and Abe lifted Matt, bringing him out of and away from the building.

The wail of the ambulance siren broke the early morning silence. The men watched as the two were evaluated, loaded and then taken away. Murphy and Ian went with them.

Caleb headed for his investigative team and spent some time with them. He then turned back to Abe.

"This is strange, Abe. How did they get here?"

Abe shrugged. "Your guess is as good as mine. Nothing has made sense with this at all."

Abe stood at Matt's bedside. He would be fine, the doctors said, just bruises and a few cuts. Matt slept again, having been awake for a while. Abe turned as Caleb entered, a frown on his face.

"How's Sarah?"

"Doug said she's fine, all things considered. Same as Matt." Caleb hesitated. "Can we talk, Abe, somewhere quiet?"

"That doesn't sound good, Caleb. Let's go to the cafeteria. It's usually fairly quiet this time of day, and I could use some food."

Trays in front of them, the two men sat at a quiet table, away from the scattered customers.

"You wanted to talk?" Abe searched his friend's face, concerned at the darkness he saw there.

"I did. Now I don't know how to approach it."

"The beginning is usually a good place."

Caleb gave a half grin, then pulled a sheet of paper out of the portfolio he carried. "This is a copy of what the crime scene team found today in the building where Matt and Sarah were."

Abe took it, apprehension flooding through him. His face grew white as he read, then his eyes raised to Caleb. "What does this mean?"

"That's what I was hoping you could tell me."

Abe read the words again:

This is just the beginning. Justice is mine and I will repay. I will not wait for the Lord to avenge me. I will be the avenger and bring you down.

"I have no idea what this is." Abe shook his head. "It could be anyone."

"That's what I was afraid you'd say. We couldn't get anything off of it." Caleb looked across the room, not focusing on anything. "This changes what happened. Now we have you as a target too. Whoever it is moved Matt and Sarah during the explosion. They're not afraid of us, to do that when so many law enforcement officials were around."

"And they found the bodies of Matt's step-grandfather and the bodyguard?"

"They did, so we know it's not them." Caleb returned his gaze to Abe. "I'm going to need you to work with our investigators on this."

"I don't understand, Caleb, but God is in control, isn't He?"

"There's a lot we don't understand this time, things that happened we don't have an explanation for or the culprit."

Epilogue

Sarah stepped back off the stepladder and folded it, ready to return it to her van.

"That's the last of the fixtures, Abe. They're really nice and suit the buildings."

"They do, don't they? Between you and Rebecca and Rachel, you've picked out some nice ones. Speaking of Rebecca, she was hoping you'd stop in on your way home."

"What's she up to know, Abe?" Sarah stowed the ladder and then reached for the equipment boxes.

"Nothing much." Abe had an amused tone to his voice.

"Abe! You know I don't like surprises."

Abe hugged her and dropped a kiss on her cheek. "Welcome to the family, Sarah."

She stepped back, mouth open as he walked away. What was he talking about? She shrugged, then pulled her van up beside the big house as they called it. She loved her home in town, but this was nice. She could handle living here, she thought.

Rebecca met her in the kitchen. "Come on, I have a dress I want you to try on. We need to do some updated photos of you."

Sarah waved her hand. "No photos, but I will

try the dress.”

Showered and garbed in an ankle-length flowing light jade dress, she studied her image in the mirror. She didn’t clean up too badly, she thought. Rebecca tapped at the door and then came in.

“It’s you, Sarah. I thought that when I saw it.” She made a circle around her friend. “The low heels are nice with it, too. Here, sit, let me do your makeup and your hair.”

Sarah sat, protesting that she hated makeup but she submitted to her friend. What was Rebecca up to?

Rebecca left, promising to be back in a minute. When a tap came at the door, Sarah expected Rebecca to enter. When she didn’t, Sarah walked over and pulled the door open.

Matt stood there, dressed in a suit, with his tie almost matching the colour of her dress. Sarah didn’t know if she had ever seen him dressed up before, and they had been dating for five months now. He reached for her hand.

“You look more beautiful than ever, Sarah. Will you have dinner with me tonight?”

She nodded, suddenly shy and at a loss for words. They walked out, not noticing Abe, Gideon and Rebecca standing watching them.

Abe sighed, “Here we go again.”

Rebecca slapped him on his arm. “Behave, Abe. One of these days, it will be you.”

Abe shook his head. “Not likely.”

After a dinner at their favourite Italian

restaurant, Matt took Sarah's hand and walked her towards the park overlooking the river. It was twilight and the stars were just starting to twinkle white in the darkening blue of the sky. He stopped her on the bridge over the river, the water trickling over the rocks in a muted musical tone.

"When I first met you, I wasn't sure about how to take you. You're a woman working in a man's world, but you have kept your feminine side. You collect people. You collected me." He turned her to him, hands resting on her shoulders. "Sarah, you have become an important part of my life. When you disappeared, I thought I had lost what I needed most. Instead, you turned me back to God, to seek His forgiveness and to learn to forgive those who had hurt me. You taught me this and helped me to seek the healing of my heart that I needed."

Matt paused, and reached to wipe a single tear from her face. "Without you, I don't think I could live my life the way God wants me to. You keep me grounded. You keep me searching in His word. Will you be mine for life, my partner, my soul mate, my best friend?"

Sarah nodded, tears sparkling in her eyes. "I will. You are that to me already."

He kissed her softly, then looked up at the sky. "I spoke with your parents. We're flying out to see them soon, your Dad asked for that."

Sarah hugged him. "Thank you. I've missed them here."

"Did you know they're thinking of moving back? They'll want their house back."

"They will, will they? What about Spider and Miss Muffet? They go with me."

Matt laughed softly. "Of course they will, though I still haven't figured out their names."

Sarah began to laugh. "Obviously your childhood was deprived. Did you never have a nursery rhyme read to you?"

Matt stared at her, his mind going back to when he was really young, ready for bed, to his mother seated in her rocking chair book open in her hands, her three children gathered around her, her husband watching from his easy chair, and then he got it. Head back, he roared with laughter as he hugged her close. Dropping a kiss on her hair, he whispered, "Only you, Sarah, could come up with names like that."

Dear Readers:

Thank you for picking up the first of a new series I have entitled *His Guardians*. It has been a challenge to write a story about forgiveness and the need to heal.

Forgiveness doesn't come easy to us. It is our nature to cling to a wrong and let it fester and grow. We need to learn how to forgive in order to heal. When we forgive, then we can let go of what caused the hurt. It doesn't change those we are forgiving. It changes us. Matt had to learn how to forgive in order to heal from past hurts. Sarah had already learned that.

The rose I mentioned in the story - my Mother always wore rose perfume. She preferred Avon's Roses Roses. When I smell the aroma of a rose, she comes to mind. I miss her so much since her graduation to heaven in 2010. I have her two roses bushes and they are cherished.

I always wanted to go into a trade. My Father was a carpenter and I wanted to follow in his footsteps. He wouldn't let me, telling me trades were too hard for a woman. That's okay. Owning my own home has allowed me to experience different parts of trades—swapping out toilets, vanities, sinks, lighting, flooring, even to changing electrical switches and outlets. It's been a fun journey updating my house to the way on want it and all on my own.

God doesn't expect us nor want us to journey all alone. He is with us every step of the way. Does He send visible angels? I believe He can and will if needed. He has provided some very good friends for me as well.

The rose pictured the front of the book is my Mom's.

God bless each one of you who has picked up this book, the first in a series of eight. I have to tell each one's story, now don't I, in order to tell Abe's? There are questions that remain unanswered in this book. They are for the telling in Abe's story. May God lead you down the path of forgiveness, if needed, to the healing only He provides.

Ronna